## "You're The Best Woman I Know, Elizabeth Brady,"

Clay said quietly. "And what I'm talking about is finding a man who's good enough for you. When you make it through this, you'll find him. The right man. A man who's good enough for a *lady*, a man who can give you what you really need and want."

Liz took a long look at Clay. Small wheels clicked in her head. All this time. All this time she'd thought Clay had pulled back from an adult relationship between them because he didn't return her feelings, because he still saw her as an honorary kid sister.

Not because he'd put her on some nonsense pedestal called "Lady."

Never because he thought he wasn't good enough for her.

Dear Reader:

Series and Spin-offs! Connecting characters and intriguing interconnections to make your head whirl.

In Joan Hohl's successful trilogy for Silhouette Desire—*Texas Gold* (7/86), *California Copper* (10/86), *Nevada Silver* (1/87)—Joan created a cast of characters that just wouldn't quit. You figure out how *Lady Ice* (5/87) connects. And in August, "J.B." demanded his own story—*One Tough Hombre*. In *Falcon's Flight*, coming in November, you'll learn *all* about . . .?

Annette Broadrick's *Return to Yesterday* (6/87) introduced Adam St. Clair. This August *Adam's Story* tells about the woman who saves his life—and teaches him a thing or two about love!

The six Branigan brothers appeared in Leslie Davis Guccione's *Bittersweet Harvest* (10/86) and *Still Waters* (5/87). September brings *Something in Common*, where the eldest of the strapping Irishmen finds love in unexpected places.

*Midnight Rambler* by Linda Barlow is in October—a special Halloween surprise, and totally unconnected to anything.

Keep an eye out for other Silhouette Desire favorites—Diana Palmer, Dixie Browning, Ann Major and Elizabeth Lowell, to name a few. You never know when secondary characters will insist on their own story. . . .

All the best,

Isabel Swift
Senior Editor & Editorial Coordinator
Silhouette Books

# JENNIFER GREENE
# Lady Be Good

## Silhouette Desire

Published by Silhouette Books New York

**America's Publisher of Contemporary Romance**

SILHOUETTE BOOKS
300 East 42nd St., New York, N.Y. 10017

ISBN: 0-373-05385-1

First Silhouette Books printing November 1987

America's Publisher of Contemporary Romance

Printed in the U.S.A.

**Books by Jennifer Greene**

Silhouette Desire

*Body and Soul* #263
*Foolish Pleasure* #293
*Madam's Room* #326
*Dear Reader* #350
*Minx* #366
*Lady Be Good* #385

---

## JENNIFER GREENE

lives near Lake Michigan. Born in Grosse Pointe, she moved to a farm when she married her husband fifteen years ago. Jennifer feels that love needs both laughter and tribulations to grow. She's won the *Romantic Times* award for sensuality and the RWA Silver Medallion, and also writes under the name of Jeanne Grant.

# One

———

"Sleep with me, Clay."

Clay was just thrusting his right arm in the sleeve of his denim jacket when he heard the distinctly feminine whisper from the couch. The silky, sleepy alto was vibrant with recklessness.

Liz Brady always did have a voice that could turn a man inside out. She also had the constitution of an ox. If there were any justice in this life, the lady would already be dead to the world. Years ago, Liz could have barely tolerated a social glass of wine, and in the past four hours he'd spiked her lemonade with enough vodka to make a Bowery bum pass out.

"Clay?"

"I heard you, honey." Smoothly, he slipped in his left arm and tugged on the rest of the jacket. The muscle in his cheek tightened when one slim, stockinged leg flexed above the back of the couch. Clay had faced more than his share of fists in a dark alley. Now he mentally extended his definition of trouble to include wriggling toes, a delicate ankle and a perfectly formed calf.

Thankfully the leg disappeared, except now her head gradually rose from the opposite side of the couch. Her face was an oval, all fine bones and fragility. Elegant white-gold hair just brushed her shoulders, reminding him of silk. Her eyes were darker than coffee and softer than rain. Liz certainly had the capacity to look like the efficient twenty-seven-year-old librarian she was, but she didn't tonight. No woman had the right to look that brazenly soft, that... crushable.

Déjà vu struck him like a torpedo. Some things a man shouldn't have to go through twice in a lifetime. The last time Liz had tried to seduce him, she'd been seventeen and prepared to sacrifice her virginity because he "needed a good woman." He figured it must have taken her months to work up the courage to buy the condoms at the local drugstore. Even at seventeen, Liz believed in being prepared.

At the moment she looked prepared for nothing, except to cause him an imminent heart attack.

"Clay..."

Whoever hired the Sirens to lure sailors on ships should have heard Liz's voice first. "I'm coming, honey." He switched off the couch lamp and moved toward her.

At seventeen, she'd been a vulnerable handful of sass, sparkle and sweetness. He'd adored her then and had never been happier than when she left for college. On the rare occasions when she'd returned to Ravensport over the past ten years, he'd carefully stayed out of her way. He'd never touched her when she was seventeen, but in his gut he knew he'd wanted to.

Years didn't change rules. Losers simply didn't touch ladies. No matter how wanton that sleepy smile or sultry those limbs, Liz was and always would be a lady. She just didn't know that at the moment.

She weaved toward him. Her pensive frown would seem to indicate a massive, monumental philosophical battle going on in her head, but something got lost when she finally reached him. "Hi," she murmured.

He almost grinned. Instead, he wrapped an arm around her shoulder before her swaying body collapsed again. "Hi back."

"The thing is—" She stopped to yawn. "I've always loved you, Clay."

"Sure you have," he said, propelling her toward the door.

Her feet rooted midway. One delicate blond brow arched up. "I seem to remember...doing this before."

"Umm-hmm."

"I was married, did you know that?"

"Yes." Her words were so slurred he could barely understand her. More than that, he was concentrating on navigating a resistant 110 pounds toward the door.

"I'm not married anymore."

"I know."

"Marriage—" she appeared to consider her choice of words—"is the pits."

"So I've heard." She still talked with her hands. Midway down the hall she did more than talk with them. She swung around in front of him and roped her arms around his neck, smoky eyes luminously raised to his, full of dance, full of darkness. Her hips initiated a gyration that raised his body temperature ten degrees.

He smoothed back the sweep of silken bangs from her forehead and tried to force a mental picture of a seventeen-year-old bookish sprite with braids. It didn't work. That child-woman had been full of pride and innocence, arousing a man's most protective instincts. The whole world had changed in ten years— the child-woman had turned all woman—but he still felt swamped by the same fierce instincts.

He never expected to run into Liz tonight. He talked with her brother, Andy, all the time, but Andy never once mentioned that Liz had gotten the divorce or that she was due home for a long stay. His visit to Andy's house was impromptu, and if he'd had better sense, he'd have left the brother and sister to their homecoming.

Clay never did have much sense. His palm touched Liz's pale cheek. She was so damn thin a breath of wind would blow her away. He'd taken one look and known she was past exhaustion and dangerously close to collapse. She hadn't known how to take off the fake smile, couldn't stop talking, couldn't stop moving her hands. Her eyes had a bruised expression, her skin was whiter than paper. Andy had given him a helpless look. He didn't have the least idea what to do with a woman trying to come apart at the seams.

Clay did, but the liquor should have worked by now. He'd spiked her lemonade because he remembered how much she used to like it. What he'd forgotten was that she was headstrong enough to defy gravity—and alcohol.

"Kiss me, Clay."

His lips obediently brushed hers. The rage billowing through him didn't transfer to her. She had a small mouth, the upper lip exactly defined, the lower one more giving. Her fragile throat arched back, inviting the pressure of a lover's kiss. His roughened thumb caressed that soft throat, calluses against flesh that bruised too easily. She tasted like citrus and smelled like spring. The man who'd put the desperation in her eyes was damn lucky not to be within a hundred miles.

"To bed," he murmured.

"Yes. Oh, Clay. I need—"

"I know exactly what you need, honey." He tucked her back under his shoulder, where he could control the walking for both of them. In heels, she was a decent height, mostly because she'd always tended toward killer stilts in shoes. In stocking feet she was pure shrimp. She was wearing a pin-striped suit in gray and coral, a coral silk blouse, coral clips in her ears. The outfit was demure, feminine and ladylike. An angel couldn't have looked more chaste.

He led the angel toward her bedroom. He knew where it was, he'd practically grown up in this house. Andy had the bedroom at the top of the stairs; Liz had the windowed room in the back that had once been a porch.

He didn't have time to turn on the light. She turned and smiled at him with total confidence, reckless urgency. Her hips made another one of those motions that would have made a monk give up the cloth. Clay had never been a monk. "You want me, don't you, Clay?" she whispered.

"Yes." He never lied to a woman in the bedroom. Besides, Liz wasn't going to remember any of this.

"You've always wanted me."

"Yes." He managed to get her suit jacket off, but then sucked in his breath when she rubbed against him like a kitten stretching in the sunshine. Carefully, gently, he moved her hands before she got into more trouble than he could handle.

"Don't worry that I'm going to be shy," she whispered.

That wasn't what he was worried about.

"I've had it with being good," she confessed. "I've had it with trying to do everything right." Moonlight bathed the dark sharp pain in her eyes. Then it was gone. "Never mind. I don't care. This time around

I'm free. I'm going to be wicked and wild. I'm going to dance on sunshine. And I'm going to seduce you this time, Clay. You're not eeling your way out of it this time. You think I can't?''

''I know you can,'' he murmured. He'd unbuttoned his share of blouses in his time, but these buttons were silk-covered and slippery, and it was dark.

''I'm not built like Mae West,'' she whispered.

''Believe me, I never cared.'' He had to undo the buttons at her cuffs before he could finally peel the blouse off her.

''How embarrassing. I'm wearing a padded bra.''

''I can see that.''

''It's nothing to do with being flat. I just hate nipples showing through clothes.''

Personally, he didn't mind them, but at the moment he wasn't following that much of her conversation. Her skin was as white as the moonlight and delectably soft. She was still built more girl than woman, a waist too small to measure, hips like a boy's, and she desperately needed weight from some solid red meat and a few lemon meringue pies.

He tried to think of lemon meringue pies. All he could think about was sex. Her body was warm, and that heat released the scent she always wore. It crossed his mind that it would have helped if she'd changed her perfume, but he realized that wasn't true. He loved her scent and he loved her skinniness. He loved that faint shadow of cleavage and he loved her chin. He adored her mouth.

He found himself staring at that mouth and waiting vaguely for guilt to hit him. She didn't have the least idea what she was doing. He didn't have any business being here, much less taking off her clothes. He felt no guilt, which told him something about honor and himself that he hadn't been quite sure of before. It wasn't that much of a surprise.

Experienced fingers glided around her skirt until he discovered the button and zipper in the back. He leaned her cheek to his chest when he managed both, and then let the coral linen skirt slide to the floor, abandoned.

The press of her small breasts and slim hips triggered a tight, hard physical response in him. He'd imagined this so many times, and her scrap of satin half-slip might as well have been nonexistent. His teeth clamped together. Blood raced through his veins.

She leaned back. It took a moment for him to figure out that she was determined to undo the buttons of his shirt. She couldn't—he doubted she could even see them. Her eyelids kept fluttering down, her legs were unsteady. Finally, that agony of tension was gone from her face.

He let her play with his shirt buttons while he leaned over and pushed aside the white quilt of the Jenny Lind couch. The pillow was in some kind of sack with ruffles; he couldn't get the sack off and manage her, too.

"Clay," she whispered huskily.

The buttons hadn't kept her busy nearly long enough. Her palms slid up his shirt, gliding up to his neck. Lightning bolted to his pulse, and like a teenage boy, his hands were suddenly slick. He tossed down the ruffled sack. To hell with it. "Slide in," he murmured softly.

"No. I want—"

"I know what you want, honey. Just give me a second to take off my clothes."

"Don't..." She hesitated, her words as slurred as her eyes were haunted with honesty. "You don't have to be careful, Clay. You don't have to be nice. I—"

"Yes. You want to be made love to, but not like a lady. Not with please and thank-you. You want to be taken until you can't think and you can't breathe and the whole damn world goes away. Believe me, sweetheart, I'd love to give you exactly what you want."

Alcohol or no alcohol, the old Liz would have been shaken at such crude bluntness. He'd counted on that, and was not prepared for her urgently whispered, "*Yes*. Give me what I want then, Clay."

Damnation. Next time, God forbid there was one, he was feeding her an entire fifth of vodka. He placed his mouth on hers with a kiss that forced her head back to the pillow. She murmured something that came close to shattering his sanity. He tucked her down into the sheets while her arms were still around his neck. Slowly then, he loosened her arms.

"Clay—"

"I'll be there. I'm just taking off my clothes. Close your eyes for a minute."

"No. I—"

"Close your eyes, Liz." His throat felt full of gravel.

He stood silent in the darkness, waiting.

Not many minutes ticked by before his sultry temptress lay still. Clay let himself out the back door. His lungs hauled in the fall night air. From the shadows of the back porch, he could see a covey of fireflies flashing in the yard in sparks of warmth and heat and light, so fast and bright, so quickly gone.

In thirty-one years, he'd never found a woman more dangerous to his equilibrium than Liz.

If she happened to remember anything that happened this night he doubted she'd ever speak to him again, which suited Clay just fine.

At four o'clock the next afternoon, Liz was in the upstairs bathroom, tipping an aspirin bottle in her palm. Her head felt like dandelion fuzz that rattled; her throat was too dry to swallow, and the brown eyes glinting back at her from the medicine cabinet mirror had interesting little red lines.

If she didn't know better, she'd think she had a hangover. Logically, it wasn't possible to have a hangover without drinking alcohol, which made her humdinger of a headache rather difficult to explain.

She swallowed two tablets and shuddered. Many, many of her recollections of the night before were difficult to explain. Several phrases jangled through her mind in reference to Clay Stewart, none of which normally passed a stable and staid twenty-seven-year-old librarian's lips. Liz, however, had left that career behind her in Milwaukee. She also had a brother downstairs who was undoubtedly wondering whether she was dead or alive.

Head pounding, she tiptoed downstairs in search of Andy. She found him, predictably, sprawled in a kitchen chair with a pile of tenth-grade math papers in front of him. Andy never changed. He still seemed about ten feet tall, and had the lanky build of a basketball player. Even on a lazy Saturday afternoon he looked like the math teacher he was—overserious, a wee bit pedantic and dressed in a blue crewneck sweater that was his favorite ten years ago.

He glanced up as she walked in. "Don't tell me the mummy finally got around to rising?"

"Something has to be wrong with all the clocks in this house," she informed him. "It couldn't conceivably be four o'clock in the afternoon."

"It is. Somebody around here slept like a whipped dog."

"Now there's an image to thrill a woman's ego." She ruffled his blond head en route to the freezer. "In spite of your insults, bro, I might be persuaded into making your dinner, assuming..." One peek inside and she leveled Andy a despairing glance. "Were you afraid there was going to be a run on pistachio ice cream? There's three gallons in here."

"I didn't know you were coming until two days ago," Andy defended.

"Don't give me that nonsense. You wouldn't have shopped if I'd given you four years' notice." By a miracle she found two packages of steaks tucked behind the ice cream and the TV dinners.

Andy's grins were as lazy as he was. "I didn't say I would have shopped. I just said I didn't have time." He added casually, "You almost look human again."

"Thanks." Her tone was wry and maybe relieved. Bantering with Andy was as comfortable as fire on a winter night.

"When you came in that door last night—"

"I know, I looked like the bride of Frankenstein. Don't rub it in. Forty-eight hours without sleep, a four-hour drive in the rain." She twisted the microwave dial to Defrost and tossed Andy a deliberately reassuring smile. She'd never meant to worry him the night before. Her brother was the best. She knew he'd stand by her in any crisis, but he was also a man who panicked if emotions entered a conversation.

"You're sure you're okay now? Because Clay seemed to think—"

"Of course I'm okay," she said briskly, "other than feeling like a spoiled brat for sleeping all day. And as for Clay..." Just the sound of his name punctured a new rattle in the dandelion fuzz upstairs. For one thing, she hadn't started drinking those lethal lemonades until Andy had slipped off to bed, certain she and Clay wanted to talk up old times. And for another..."Never mind Clay." The microwave pinged, and two steaks were suddenly begging to be marinated. "Listen, bro. As I told you on the phone, I'm considering a move back here, but that doesn't have to mean right here. I want you to be frank with me, because if I'll be in your way—''

''Try not to be more of an idiot than you already are, would you? Last I knew, this was your home just as much as it's mine.''

Her chin firmed. ''You're thirty-one and have been used to your privacy for a long time. Maybe there's someone in your life.''

''Thousands of women, banging on the door nightly,'' Andy agreed laconically. ''Still, I believe we can work out an arrangement where you wouldn't be too much in the way.'' With a catcher's ease he caught the towel she hurled teasingly at his head. ''Try and get it through your head that you're welcome, would you, sis? Although if you're worried about it, you could take on all the cooking. And the laundry. And the—''

''Did you say you wanted your steak charred black?''

''Hey, I was joking.'' He added gruffly, ''You short on cash?''

''Nope. You?''

''Always.'' He shuffled the papers on the table to one side. ''Finally get that divorce business straightened out with the creep?''

''Signed, sealed and delivered two days ago.'' Her tone could have won an award for easy cheer.

''About time. Damn!''

''What?''

''I forgot Michigan was playing Notre Dame this afternoon. I bet I've missed the first two quarters.''

"Oh, no." Liz slammed her palm to her forehead. "The world will come to an end. Life's over. The whole day's ruined. How will we survive?"

"For reasons I can't imagine," Andy said irritably from the doorway, "I've missed you."

Liz had missed him just as much. The tough subjects had already been opened and closed as far as Andy was concerned. That suited her just fine, and no one on earth was as easy to be with as her brother. As if ten years hadn't passed, they bantered through dinner, argued over dishes and flopped on opposite couches in the den to watch a Saturday night movie.

After Andy went to bed, she found herself restlessly wandering from room to room, letting the silence and solitude of really being home wash over her. So little had changed. The chime clock in the front hall still ran four minutes slow. The fourth step on the stairs still creaked. The den was still crowded with newspapers and afghans and half-read books.

Forty-eight hours before the instinct to come home had been fierce, fast and unstoppable. Receiving her divorce decree had been the catalyst. A stranger might have considered that irrational, when the marriage had died more than a year before the legal system acknowledged it so. A stranger might also have considered it irrational for her to suddenly pack up, turn the key on her Milwaukee apartment, and use her vacation in lieu of notice on the safe, secure job she'd held for more than five years.

She'd desperately wanted to immediately come home. It wouldn't wait. The whole world was welcome to judge her actions as irrational. Liz knew better. Coming home was the best decision she'd made in ten years.

She paused in front of the picture window in the living room. She could see the neighborhood she'd grown up in, the shaded yards and kids' swing sets and the porches where people still sat out on a summer night.

It was odd, but one could smell Ravensport. It smelled like families, like something that lasted. Like people who loved a good gossip and panicked over gas prices but had a hard time relating those to trouble in the Middle East because world affairs were so far away. What mattered was putting food on the table, affording that new car, Johnny's braces. Ravensport smelled like real life.

When the hall clock chimed midnight, Liz was still wandering, still touching things. Memories of her growing-up years haunted every room, some good, some unsettling. But she hadn't come home because she thought it would be easy.

The last time she'd lived here she'd been seventeen, innocent as the green grass, headstrong, confident and terribly angry inside. Andy had been her guardian during her last year in high school. After their divorce, both parents had assumed she'd live with one of them. They were dead wrong and, at the time, no one was in a hurry to light the emotional powder keg of the teenager she'd suddenly turned into.

Except Clay Stewart, of course.

If last night's memories of Clay were on hold, Liz almost smiled as older memories sprang into her head. She could still remember Clay's long arm blocking her passage out of the small downstairs bathroom off the kitchen. "If you seriously think you're going out with that smooth dude in tight jeans, you're out of your tree."

She recalled another scene in the dining room; she was dressed in senior prom finery that contrasted to his scuzzy jeans and frayed sweatshirt. "Clay, the *entire senior class* is staying out all night."

"Then the entire senior class can escort you back home by one," he'd told her.

And right after her parents' divorce, she could remember sitting on the back porch with him. Actually, she hadn't been sitting. She'd been lying on her back, wearing cutoffs, her bare feet propped up on the porch pillar, and the fireflies had been darting in and out of the summer night. He'd never interrupted her extremely mature monologue about how stupid marriage was, how even more stupid love was, and from everything the kids had to say she'd figured out that sex rated up there with worthless. He'd said nothing until she was done, and then he'd wrapped his arms around her in a massive bear hug and murmured, "Whether you believe it or not, you're going to forgive your parents sometime. You're also going to stop worrying that it was your fault. There was nothing you could do, Liz, it was just them. You want to be angry, you go ahead. I'm right here."

At seventeen, Liz had been so in love with Clay that she couldn't think straight. He was always there when she needed someone. He always understood. On the surface, Clay Stewart was the last man on earth to turn into a tough honorary guardian, no matter how long he'd been friends with her brother. No one in Ravensport had ever been in as much trouble as him. His mother drank and no one knew who his father was. He was arrested twice for reckless driving. When the mayor's daughter got pregnant, she pointed the finger at Clay, and what a scandal ensued when he wouldn't marry the girl. He was always in a fight. All Clay had to do was breathe and there was trouble.

Liz knew all of that, but she'd known better. As a kid, Clay had always worn a leather jacket, walked with a lazy swagger and had a dangerously sexy gleam in his eyes. The whole town saw him as arrogant, belligerent and tough. She saw him as a lonely man who desperately needed someone to understand and believe in him.

The hall clock chimed two. Liz climbed the stairs for bed suddenly recalling that last night was the second time in her life that she'd tried—and failed—to seduce Clay Stewart.

She undressed in the dark and slid between cool white sheets. Clay had rejected her with all the delicacy of a brick the first time. He told her he'd shoot her if she ever tied up with a loser like him.

She hadn't tied up with a loser. She'd left home and gone to college and tied up with David. The quick, painful streak of rebellion that had haunted her senior year of high school disappeared. She wasn't by nature a rebel. She'd reestablished relationships with her parents; she'd grown up and pursued a stable career. When she finally married David, there had never been any possibility she'd end up in a divorce. She'd entered into marriage intending never to give it the chance to fail.

Only now she seemed to be divorced. And her marriage had definitely failed.

Through the window, she could see gray clouds scuttling past the white cradle of a moon. Leaves rustled against the pane in a restless wind. Sleep refused to come.

She hadn't come home for Clay. She hadn't come home for any man. Lingering feelings for David were no longer an issue, but despair had weighed down her life for more than a year. She couldn't seem to get back any faith in herself as a woman. As a teenager, she'd been foolish, impulsive, stubborn and blindly angry at what had happened to her parents. She'd built up a whole existence making sure it wouldn't happen to her. In real life one shelved emotions if one wanted to be safe, and Liz had pursued a stable career and stable man with ruthless intensity.

It was a heck of a way to live but it seemed to have taken her ten years to discover that a woman who lied to herself had a hard time looking in a mirror. Somewhere inside Liz Brady was an honest woman. She'd come home to find her again.

Images of Clay and last night filled her mind. She tested her conscience for embarrassment, guilt, horror, shame, and found appropriate amounts of each. Still, those weren't the only emotions she discovered. Clay had made a serious error in judgment the night before. It wasn't in spiking her lemonade, but in crossing the path of a woman on a collision course with honesty. Clay was part of a time in her life when she'd taken emotion and love and trust for granted.

The old Liz, after throwing herself at him like a runaway freight train, would be tempted to bury her head in the nearest sand and meticulously avoid him for the next 187 years or so. Pride had always been important to her, far more important than honesty.

The new Liz hadn't come home to hide, but to come to terms.

She had to face Clay again.

# Two

---

Rain pattered against the windows as Clay stood up and tossed his reading glasses onto the cluttered desk. The glare of car lights flashed brightness in the gloomy night. Rain inevitably brought business to the motel, and judging from the congested parking lot, the night's receipts were going to be outstanding.

He wished he could give a hoot.

Itchy and restless, he pushed out of the desk chair. The teak desk was pretty fancy for a man wearing old denims and a frayed white shirt. Both the desk and the paperwork made him feel like a fraud, a player at success. He thought of himself as a man with a losing poker hand who still put money in the pot in the hope he could outbluff his opponents.

Dragging a hand impatiently through his hair, he identified his mood as sour. This same mood had been pushing at him for the past five days. A good fistfight would have relieved some of the excess dark energy; so would driving a Maserati at a hundred miles an hour on a mountain curve, or a nice roaring drunk.

It would also have helped if Liz Brady weren't back in town. It would have helped even more if he hadn't touched her.

What he really needed was a tiger to wrestle. Not too many of those were running around Ravensport, Wisconsin. He crossed the stone-gray carpet to his son's room and silently opened the door. That fast, his bad temper eased into a blend of humor and helplessness.

Clay's own two rooms were dominated by grays and creams and austerity. The lack of knickknacks talked up a man's refusal to depend on possessions. He could have packed up everything he owned in a matter of hours.

What Spence jammed in his room would take a semi to move. Four-gallon aquariums bargained for space with schoolbooks. Stuffed animals had been miraculously reproducing in the far corner for years. Lego spacecraft had taken over the closet and a floor-to-ceiling shelf unit was jammed with collections— books, coins, comics, bits of glass. Spence never threw anything out.

He was also supposed to be asleep by eight-thirty. The room was dark, but not so dark Clay couldn't make out the bottoms-up bundle under a mound of covers. The tattletale beam of light peeking through the blankets told its own story.

The feeling of love washed through Clay, fierce, thick and as powerful as any emotion he'd ever known. He had to force sternness into his voice. "Hey. I thought I told you to put out the light a half hour ago."

Two layers of comforters pushed back to reveal a flashlit freckled face, a disheveled mop of brown hair and disgusted brown eyes. "Dad, I've told you and told you. No one can stop reading *Encyclopedia Brown* in the middle of a chapter. You have to know what happens."

"You want to find out what happens if I catch you reading by flashlight again? How many times do I have to tell you you're going to wreck your eyes?" Clay strode forward and started retucking sheets and blankets. "I'm going out on the floor for a while. Cameron will be in the next room and you've got the beeper if you need me."

"I don't need the beeper anymore. Hell, I'm eight years old!"

"You're never going to make it to nine if you don't quit that swearing."

The threat, like all of Clay's threats, never produced more than a cheeky grin from his son. "Sure, Dad."

Clay considered giving him the good swat on the bottom he certainly deserved, but instead he reached over to brush his son's cheek. Spence's small fingers curled around his neck in a viselike hug, and all

thought of discipline disappeared. His son smelled like
warm milk and toothpaste and crayons. Damn, but he
loved those smells. "Now, go to sleep," he said
gruffly.

Seconds later, he closed the bedroom door and
waited for the full mental count of twenty. "Turn off
the light," he called through the door.

"For cripes sake! It's just two more paragraphs!"

"Now, Spence." Soon Clay was going to establish
authority in their father-son relationship.

"Okay, okay."

As Clay let himself out into the motel corridor, the
dark mood jumped back on him like a flea on a hound
dog. He wasn't a fit father for Spence.

All his life he'd specialized in doing the wrong thing.
Spence's mother had been one of Clay's worst mistakes. Mary had been around the block a few times, a
dark-haired temptress looking for a fast affair. She
wasn't really different from most of the women who'd
wandered through his life—but Mary had lied about
being prepared. She'd also told him to go to hell when
he proposed marriage.

He'd felt rage when she was killed in a car crash, not
because of Mary, but because the local authorities had
placed his infant son in foster care. He'd quickly discovered that an unwed father had no legal rights, and
what exactly Ravensport felt about Clay Stewart's
qualifications to be a single parent.

For two years his son had been in that place.

In those same two years, Clay had scraped together
the down payment for the motel. At the time, the place

had a reputation for bad wiring, bad food and no-questions-asked accommodations. The lobby decor had been limited to cracked vinyl couches and a gum-chewing clerk.

Now, on the surface, the look of his brightly lit lobby identified success. A fire blazed in the corner hearth, plants accented the oak paneling, and wet, tired travelers were taking advantage of the comfort-able grouping of chairs and couches. However, fancy teak desks and oak paneling didn't erase a man's mis-takes, and couldn't change who a man was or where he'd been.

Clay checked in with Cameron, then Susie at the front desk, then stalked through the kitchen and res-taurant and took his broodiness to the bar.

The dark lighting and secluded booths usually soothed a round of bad temper. If that failed, Char could be counted on to raise his blood pressure if not his attitude. Even though she was behind the piano he could see she was dressed in her usual outfit of some-thing outlandish and low-cut enough to push legal standards of decency. Her sultry wink didn't work to-night. There was a problem with establishing a place designed for the restless, the lonely, the angry-with-no-place-to-put-it. The problem was that he fit in, per-fectly.

Wandering behind the bar counter, he automati-cally filled a draft for a waiting customer. At the far end, George was polishing glasses. Five foot ten and built like a Sherman tank, George could listen to more troubles in an evening than a practicing psychiatrist.

George took an annoyingly shrewd look at his boss, then motioned toward the filled tables. "Quiet as a tomb."

"I can see that." Clay skimmed the room on the off chance there might be one potential drunk, one potential troublemaker. Undoubtedly because the bar had his name on it, the townspeople assumed it specialized in action and excitement. Even after all these years, Ravensport still loved to believe the worst of him. Most of the time, Clay found high humor in making money based on his reputation, particularly when the highest excitement in the place was the dip in Char's neckline. Tonight, though, he would have appreciated a good slug of decent trouble.

"Spence run you ragged?" George asked him.

"Spence always runs me ragged. The kid terrifies me. How is it possible for a man who barely finished high school to have a bookaholic eight-year-old son learning algebra?"

"S-o-o-o...." George tossed down his towel. "Is that what's been eating at you all week?"

"Nothing's been eating at me all week that a sock in the jaw wouldn't cure," Clay said dryly.

"You looking for volunteers?"

"I imagine you'd be in the first line-up. You don't have to tell me that I've been ornerier than a bear to work with."

"I've seen you worse. Just not often. Have you tried castor oil?"

Clay responded with the appropriate gesture, and George chuckled. Rapping his knuckles on the bar,

Clay prepared to leave when his eyes were drawn to the woman just entering the doorway.

Fine, silvery hair floated straight from her shoulders, still glistening with rain. She was wearing ice-blue slacks and a matching loose-knit sweater that swallowed her slim figure. The gleam of pink on her lips was her only claim to makeup. The demure pastels accented the unspoken label of "lady."

A single glance at her made Clay's stomach tighten. Desire as intense and fast as bad news shot through him. In three seconds flat, he had a name for the restlessness that had been dictating his mood for the past five days.

Pausing in the doorway, acting as if she owned the world, her gaze whisked interestedly through the bar, landed on Clay and passed right on.

Clay found his mouth starting to twitch in an unwilling grin. She wandered toward the bar and slid on the stool directly in front of him. If he was in the same universe, she wasn't letting on. She looked right at George, not at him, until George sidled forward with a towel draped over his arm. "What'll it be, miss?"

"A spiked lemonade, please," she said demurely.

A frog jumped into Clay's throat, threatening to choke him. George passed him a curious look. "Pardon?"

"If you're not familiar with the drink, I believe the devil next to you is." Her slim hand extended across the counter to George. "I'm Liz Brady. I know I haven't met you before, but I was born and raised in the area. This place used to be pure seed. You've done a fantastic job with it!''

"I have," George agreed blandly. His handshake across the counter identified an instant conspirator, and then he settled elbows on the counter. "For the compliment, you get one on the house, but you might have to tell me the components of a spiked lemonade.''

"I'll take care of the lady, George."

Liz noted that she seemed to be sliding off the bar stool, abetted helpfully by Clay's hand locked on the back of her neck.

She glanced up, eyes dancing and heart quaking. After five days, it was fairly obvious the mountain wasn't coming to Mohammed. Knowing she had to face him was one thing, but a grown woman who'd behaved like a nymphomaniac had needed a few days to build up courage. She'd thought she'd done that, but all her courage seemed to have stalled in the doorway.

That first night, she'd had high hopes her reactions to Clay had been colored by alcohol. One glance, however, and her pulse started clicking just as hard and fast as it had ten years ago.

Clay still had the strong bones of a Viking, the dark eyes of a hawk and a head of thick, fox-blond hair that defied the tame of a brush. His brows went every which way. Sharp cheekbones and a damn-the-world chin were set in a square face with a Roman blade of a nose. The lines around his eyes and brow mapped the experience of a man who'd lived hard, played hard and intended to do more of both. When angered his mouth could set in a cruel slash.

Adjectives like "nice" and "handsome" might as well stay home. The blunt bold features were exactly what drew a woman's attention, and the female population of Ravensport had never cared that he wasn't pretty. His clothes had always been a blatant statement of sexuality. His eyes dared a woman to tame him. He didn't use fancy after-shaves or men's colognes to draw a woman's attention. He breathed. That was enough.

At least it had always been enough for Liz. Her galloping pulse was a familiar feeling, and so was the way he looked at her. Those dark eyes still glinted with humor and exasperation, as if he had a lovable puppy on his hands who was undoubtedly going to make a puddle. She could have sworn Clay had kissed her a few nights ago as if he'd finally realized she was older than jailbait.

The instant they stepped into the bright lobby, he dropped his hand from her nape faster than a hot potato. "Well? I had some doubts we were on talking terms."

She looked up so her gaze met his. She'd let on about her nervousness when the ground turned into sky. "That's what I came to find out. Have any other women draped themselves all over you lately?"

He fought the grin but it surfaced. "None as sassy as you always were." His gaze dredged over her head to toe, not assessing her as a woman might like to be assessed, but as if he were checking a mud-playing toddler for damages. "You look better," he judged critically.

"I've heard more overwhelming compliments."

"If you're expecting an apology, you're not going to get one."

"Fine. If you're expecting me to make another pass at you, you can forget that, too. Now can we get off that subject and get onto something interesting. Like, does an old friend get a tour of this place or do I have to nose around all on my own?" She glanced around. "This place is pretty high class for a man who used to be hell-bent for trouble. I'm not going so far as to admit I'm impressed, mind you, but . . ."

Clay hesitated less than a second. His better sense had been warning him to stay away from her for the past five days. He still intended to do just that, as soon as he was absolutely positive she was all right.

He swung an arm around her shoulder the way he'd done a thousand times when she was younger. Her scent, which he ignored, reminded him of butterflies and yellow roses. Her hip momentarily grazed his and a sexual charge volted through his blood. He ignored that, too. "You'd be impressed by anything I did when it rains cats," he said dryly. "Come on, sunshine. You'll get your tour."

He took her to the restaurant kitchen first. While she sampled chocolate mousse and poked around his cupboards and chatted with his cooks, he studied her with ruthless intensity. She'd obviously rested; the dark circles were gone from beneath her eyes, but she was still too thin. The sass and sparkle were part of the

child-woman he remembered, but her smiles hinted of
shadows and her eyes were a haunting brown.

He kept looking, wanting to see changes that just
weren't there. The woman was far more potent than
the girl he'd felt drawn to protect. Liz was so damned
good. Her pastel softness, her vulnerability, the feminine, giving quality so natural to her. Through the
years, he'd ruthlessly avoided women of that breed.
Rogues didn't mess with ladies, and Clay had no intention of messing with Liz. Only he wanted to see her
happy, and dammit, she wasn't.

She poked her head in his freezer rooms, broom
closets and cupboards like a kitten let loose for the
first time. He lost her briefly, until he realized she'd
stepped out of the kitchen. Slim hands on hips, her
gaze rippled over the crowded room of diners, the
well-stocked salad and dessert bars, the draperies
drawn against a night flashing lightning.

The decor wasn't fancy, but the red carpet and Tif-
fany-style table lamps promoted a quiet serenity.
When their eyes met her lips curved in a satisfied
smile. "You've done it, haven't you?"

"Done what?"

"They're all here. Grissom and his family over in
the corner—there was a time he would have been
happy to run you out of town. And I don't know if
Curtis is still police chief, but you two were hardly
friends ten years ago." She named others, and then
simply motioned to the room in general. "This place
used to be nothing. A hangout for trouble, maybe a
place for truckers to stop at in a snowstorm." She

shook her head, and said softly, "You've showed them all, Clay. It's got to feel good."

His grin took a cynical twist. "Obviously you're more easily impressed than you used to be. I hate to tell you, but if I showed you the mortgage on this place, I'd be scraping you up off the floor."

She paid no attention. Laughter danced in her eyes as she gave him a critical head-to-toe, taking in the white shirt and the jeans that were such a direct contrast to the restaurant patrons' more formal dress. "You still look pretty rough and tough. What a fake."

"You didn't have any illusions I'd ever turn into the suit and briefcase type?" She was making him uncomfortable. He steered her away from the noise and bustle of the restaurant and kitchens.

"But you've turned into the father type, haven't you? Andy said you had a son." The news still disturbed her. However infrequently she'd been back home, however in character it was for her brother to avoid talking about other people's affairs, it seemed impossible to Liz that she couldn't have known Clay had a child. From the quick fierce glow in his eyes, she knew instantly how much that child mattered to him.

"Yes, I have a son. Spence."

"Is he like you?"

"No, thank God," Clay said wryly.

Her eyes searched his. "I don't know what that's supposed to mean, but I think he'd be doing pretty well if he turned out like you."

"In and out of trouble half his life, you mean? Forget it. That kid's going to keep his nose clean or I'll

die trying.'' He didn't want to talk about himself or
Spence. ''You didn't mention how long you were
staying in town.''

''I haven't any idea.'' She added smoothly, ''What
was she like?''

''Who?''

''Spence's mother.''

He paused, the half-amused, half-exasperated glint
in his eyes suggesting she'd crossed the line between
the curiosity implicit between old friends and down-
right prying. ''I don't know why you're asking the
questions. I can see from your eyes that you've already grilled your brother.''

''I have,'' she agreed wryly.

''So what's there to say? It all happened a long time
ago. I got a girl pregnant, which surprised no one in
this town. She wouldn't marry me, which surprised no
one, either. Push came to shove when she died and her
father had the nerve to stash the kid in a foster home.
I discovered damn fast that an unmarried father has
no legal rights. It took me two years in and out of
court to get him. This town had some pretty strong
feelings about Clay Stewart's qualifications as a father. And if you've been asking questions around, I
expect you already knew all that. Did you think you'd
hear a prettier version of the story if you heard it from
me? Because there is no pretty version. That's exactly
the way it was.''

She heard the old clipped defensiveness in his tone,
and briefly considered shaking him. Silver knives of
rain sliced against the glass panes of the corridor

where they'd been walking. Even the lightning looked cold, white cold, against the bleak night.

A long time ago her instincts had been to wrap her arms around Clay and shelter him against a life riddled with too many endlessly bleak, cold nights. The old instinct was still there. He'd always been hard on himself, unforgiving, harsh. He'd also always made an effort to make her think the worst of him. He used to tell her she had to stop seeing the world through rose-colored glasses, especially where that world applied to him.

If he wanted her to see him as a cold-blooded man who'd desert a pregnant girl, he had a long wait coming. That stark picture didn't match the man she knew and never would. From the time Andy had told her the story, pictures had filled her head. She'd envisioned Clay involved with a woman who didn't care for him, of Clay fighting for his son, of a younger Clay who'd seemed so doomed for trouble, with no one ever there for him.

"Another time maybe you'll feel like talking about it," she said quietly.

"There's nothing to talk about. I just told you." He pushed an impatient hand through his hair.

"Yes." There were times she'd slap that chip off his shoulder, and times when she'd wanted to love him so hard he'd have to believe he wasn't alone in the world. He'd make something of himself—she'd always known he would—only no one seemed to have told Clay. The aloofness was still there. He still wasn't inviting anyone in—least of all her.

After ten long years, how could she have expected anything else? She took a breath, and focused belatedly on the empty corridor. "Where is it we're headed, anyway?" she asked lightly.

"I was taking you back toward my place, but I didn't realize . . ." He glanced at his watch. "It's later than I thought."

Her spine stiffened instantly. "And you obviously have work to do in the evenings. I didn't mean to take up so much of your time." Her hand tightened on her jacket and purse as she started for the door at the far end of the corridor. She shouldn't have pried—darn it, where had she parked her car?—and after a decade you'd think she could have broken a long-standing habit of making herself a nuisance around Clay Stewart.

"Last I noticed, this was just a hall, not a racetrack."

"Like you said, it's late." He certainly wanted her gone; his stride matched her pace toward the exit sign. "You're going to let me meet your Spence sometime?" she asked lightly.

"Sure."

When they reached the door, Liz glanced out to a parking lot as black as wet onyx and yellow yard lights making prisms in the downpour. As fast as possible, she tugged on her jacket. "It's not only raining cats and dogs, it looks cold out there," she murmured casually.

"Liz."

She tilted her face up, and then he didn't know what to say. He had to resist the urge to zip up the jacket, raise the collar, touch her. One short hour with Liz and his stomach was tied in knots.

He wanted her both to go and to stay. He wanted to tell her about Spence, but he didn't want her to know about the things he'd done in his life that he was ashamed of. He was proud of the success he'd made of the motel, and hoped she'd see that he'd changed. But in his gut, he knew he hadn't changed. He was still Clay Stewart and would never be the kind of man who belonged in her life.

Only he'd had his hour, and dammit, Liz-style, she'd managed to probe into his life. He'd totally failed to probe into hers, all that mattered. "Andy said you'd just quit a job," he came up with finally.

"Yes."

"So... you're thinking about settling back here?"

She finished zipping up the jacket, tugged her purse straps to her shoulder and slugged her hands in her pockets. Seconds before, she could have sworn he wanted her out of his hair—and life. Now he leaned back against the cool stone of the vestibule, legs jutting out and arms folded as if ready for a siege of talk. "I came home to see if I could find work," she admitted.

"What kind of work?"

"Selling popcorn, waiting tables, pushing a broom." Her tone was wry. "I'm a qualified industrial librarian—that's what I've been doing for the past five years."

"So what does an industrial librarian do?"

"Clay—"

"I mean it. I want to know."

She sighed. "Most high tech companies have been computerized for years, but computers don't necessarily make information easily available to the people who need it. Fast access to information can mean the difference between profit and loss, so an industrial librarian's job is to organize, reference, develop systems that make access to information easier. Look, Clay, you're busy, and I'd better be—"

"Maybe the rain will let up if you wait a minute." He continued smoothly, "Sounds like that kind of job would be right up your alley. You always loved books."

"Too much. It's called hiding from life, one of several habits I'm working on breaking lately. To heck with it. This time around I'll sell popcorn." She gave him a rueful smile and expected one in return. Instead Clay's mouth was set in a line and his gaze fastened on her face with a searing intensity, intimate intensity that shook her.

The rain kept beating down just feet away. The shadowed corridor was populated by no one. The small square vestibule had the isolated feeling of an island. She'd felt that sensation of the two of them alone and the world be damned years ago, but this was different. The look in his eyes was lonely, hungry, possessive. She felt the pull of a strong man's magic, the unique brand of intimacy in honesty that rarely happens between a man and a woman and can only happen between a man and a woman.

"How bad was it?" he asked quietly.

"What?"

"The divorce."

Her fingers curled inside her coat pockets. She faced him with eyes too bright, a chin tilted at a stubborn angle. "You don't still have to play big brother."

"Who's playing big brother? You suddenly too old to need a friend?"

"Never that." She tried to smile.

She tried so hard it broke his heart. "The bastard cheated on you, didn't he?"

Something about his familiar low, gruff tenor came close to making her eyes fill with tears. She made a helpless gesture, struggling to find the right thing to say. Pride suddenly became confused in her mind with the honesty she wanted to express. "Don't waste any tea and sympathy, Clay. Whatever my ex-husband did, it opened my eyes to mistakes I was making, wrong choices I'd taken. In certain ways, the divorce has been the best thing that ever happened to me. I needed to make some changes in my life and that's exactly what I'm doing. I'm absolutely fine."

She couldn't have been more startled to see Clay suddenly coming toward her. Her hands were still clenched in her pockets when his arms wrapped her up and squeezed, heart-achingly hard.

"What are you—?"

"Don't get any ideas this is pity, short stuff. This is a simple life-is-a-bitch hug. There was a time you and I used to share quite a few of them."

"Yes." Ten years' distance washed away in the tick of a second. She remembered his bone-crunching hugs like yesterday, complete with the beat of his heart, the warmth of him, the power of muscle and Clay's big hands.

Her arms slipped around him and her cheek snuggled under his chin. Desire flowed through her veins, inevitable from the contact of thigh to thigh and breast to breast—at least, inevitable for her with Clay. That first night home, she'd been afraid she'd destroyed any potential for rebuilding a relationship with Clay that had once been irretrievably precious to her.

When he severed the contact, she was smiling. The smile turned into a chuckle when he tilted up her chin and zipped her jacket to her throat as if he was sending a kid out into a snowstorm.

"You got something for your head?"

"No."

He glanced ruefully at the rain, then back at her with a mock scowl. "You never did have the sense to own a hat."

"Neither did you."

"But then I'm tough and you're still no bigger than a minute." He touched her nose with the tip of his finger. "On your way home, don't be accepting any lemonades from men you don't know."

She appeared to consider. "I don't know, Clay. I've always loved lemonade."

"Would you kindly get out of here so I can get some work done?"

His lazy smile disappeared as he watched her race pell-mell through the rain-slick parking lot. He'd never meant to hug her, never meant to touch her at all. He knew that exposure to yellow roses was lethal to him, but all he could think of was the bastard who'd hurt her.

I'm absolutely fine, she'd said. Fine? Faster than lightning she was talking about throwing a career to the winds, moving on a whim, changing her whole life. That first night home, he'd seen firsthand how fine she was. Liz was light, sunshine, sweetness—everything that was good in life, everything that was vulnerable. He'd give five years for five short minutes with her ex-husband.

He'd settled for a hug. It was a sixty-second chance to be a wall between Liz and life, between Liz and that haunting sadness in her eyes. That wasn't so unforgivable.

He had to face the truth. You touched her because you wanted her, he thought. Because you've always wanted her. Leave her alone. You can see she's vulnerable as glass right now.

Liz had always been a lady for white knights, not black ones. Her car was gone and the rain still drizzled down while he stood there.

# Three

───

The leaves swirled about Liz's ankles as she walked home from town. Every tree lining the neighborhood street appeared to be on fire with sun-dipped colors of russet and amber, apricot and gold. Picture windows had pinups of skeletons and pumpkins in anticipation of Halloween. Someone was burning leaves—undoubtedly against an ordinance, but darn it, who cared? The smell was delicious.

Her step was swinging until she reached the tall fence surrounding the elementary school grounds. She paused then. Girls were jumping rope; the boys had a football in the air. Laughter and children's shouts seemed to float suspended in the sun. Liz could remember recesses and waiting for a turn on the tall steel swings as if it were yesterday.

She'd been home two weeks and kept waiting for the little nagging voices of depression to hit. What are you doing shuffling through leaves when you don't have a job, Liz? Aren't you getting a little worried about the state of your bank account?

Well, she was a little worried. She was also taking walks, something she hadn't done in ten years. Other improvements included sleeping until she wasn't exhausted anymore, eating with an honest appetite, remembering how the sunshine felt on her face, seeing old friends, trying new things. Life was such a terribly precious commodity. How had she let herself forget that for so long?

Her ex-husband's face flashed in front of her mind. She thought of David, and of all the friends she'd gone to school with. Many of them had married fresh out of high school with stars in their eyes and dreams of happily-ever-afters. She'd believed she knew better than to make that mistake. Her parents had loved each other and their lives had still been torn up in divorce. A relationship obviously didn't take love to make it work. It took effort, compromise. She'd married a good man and had had every intention of making him a good wife.

She'd tried. She'd ironed his shirts and combed through cookbooks, listened to symphonies and taken up jogging, all because she wanted to be a good wife to David. She hated ironing, cooking, classical music and sweating. Always had.

At the time, she'd thought all the little white lies were necessary. She'd thought she was facing life, was doing what she had to do to make a marriage work. The woman had to be the giver.

Except that she'd never fathomed that the price of despair would be so high. The little lies were never supposed to add up to a total sacrifice of emotional honesty. The bottom line for Liz had been discovering exactly how hard it was night after night to sleep with a man she didn't love.

When she discovered David had been sleeping with someone else, her first reaction had been overwhelming hurt and disillusionment. Her second had been relief. It was over. David had fought the divorce for more than a year, insisting they still had a marriage worth fighting for. He'd told her he wouldn't have strayed if she hadn't been so cold.

She'd certainly been an unforgivable liar, but she wasn't cold.

Liz closed her eyes, feeling the beat of healing sun on her face, the soothing rustle of leaves behind her head. Guilt had dogged her footsteps for a year. The guilt was deserved, but one could wallow in that forever. It didn't help. She'd made a very bad mistake, but the only possible way to correct it was to make sure it didn't happen again.

She'd never felt less safe in her life, dawdling through the past two weeks with no security, no job, and nothing but a sagging bank account to hold on to. She was scared witless...but determination was growing. She'd played it safe forever. No more.

A football soared over the school fence, and a dozen boys suddenly rushed toward her. With a grin, she fetched their ball and tossed it back, and only then noticed a small boy in the middle of their group. He was maybe eight or nine.

The freckles on his nose glinted in the sun. His head was a mop of light brown hair. His untied Reeboks were crisscrossed and there was a giant book on his lap. The football whizzed back and forth over his head, feet trampling all around him. He never budged. Once, patiently, he raised his hand to avert an imminent head-bump from the ball.

Liz knew as sure as she was born that he was Clay's son. Not because he was reading—Clay had never picked up a book in school unless he'd had to—but there was something about the child. The stubbornness of a kid pursuing what he wanted to do in spite of the crowd. The way he sat there and ignored danger. His isolation—his determination to be part of the others but not really, not quite—was another clue.

The recess bell produced a chorus of protests and stampeding feet toward the school doors. The little one lurched to his feet, still holding his book open. She couldn't resist calling out, "Spence?"

He turned curiously, brown eyes squinting in the sun. He had his father's dark chocolate eyes and damn-the-world chin and instant wariness. "You know me?"

"No." She shook her head. "I know your father, and when I saw you I was sure you were Clay's son."

"Clay's my dad's name, but I don't talk to strangers."

"You shouldn't," she agreed, abruptly feeling foolish—and wrong—for calling him. "I just wanted to meet you, to say hello." She felt increasingly like an idiot. "I know you have to get back in."

"Yeah, there's hell to pay around here if you're late." He waved. "See you around."

She blinked at his language, then a grin touched her lips as she watched him. He ambled for the door at his own pace, his step cocky in spite of his untied shoes, his jacket carelessly open in spite of the cool day. He was definitely Clay's son.

There was something about the Stewart men. On sight, given less than sixty seconds of conversation, she'd fallen in love with the eight-year-old child. And one of those honesties she was painfully trying to face and cope with was that after ten long years' absence, she'd still never quite managed to fall out of love with his father.


As soon as Clay stepped out of the car, he heard the distinct sound of swear words. Zipping his jacket against the cold wind, he wandered toward the yellow lights of the garage. The colorful epithets seemed to be emanating from beneath a rust heap of a car. All Clay could immediately see were Andy's long legs stretched out on the cement.

"Need a hand?"

Andy slid out, the black on his face and hands as dour as his scowl. "What I need is a new car."

"I've been telling you that for four years."

"This time I'm serious."

"I've heard that one before, too."

"I figured I'd get this done by 'Monday Night Football,' and instead—what time is it?"

"Close to halftime."

"That does it." Andy lurched to his feet and grabbed a rag for his hands. "Come on in. I'll get us a beer."

As soon as Clay stepped in the kitchen, a week-old headache intensified. The place looked transformed since the night Liz had arrived. A vase of yellow asters sat on the kitchen table; a pink sweater was folded over a chair. No dirty dishes cluttered the sink and the whole house smelled like furniture polish. She'd completely annihilated one of the last honest bachelor bastions in Ravensport.

She also wasn't there. Not that Clay hadn't dropped in on Andy a zillion times over the past dozen years to share a beer and "Monday Night Football," but he'd expected her to be home.

"Dallas is playing. Should be a good game." Andy popped the top and handed Clay a beer he didn't want.

"Fine. Where is she?" Clay asked casually.

"Liz?" Andy led the way to the den. "Tracking my sister these days is like trying to catch a firefly," he said dryly. "I'm not sure I remember what she's doing tonight. I guess just a movie." He flipped on the set and dropped to the closest chair, leaning forward with his legs far apart in the stance of every honorary arm-chair coach.

Clay watched long enough to catch the score. "Alone?" he asked finally.

Andy glanced up. "Alone what?"

"Did she go to the movie alone?"

"Look at that kick!"

"Yeah." Clay slugged down three gulps of the beer. There was no rousing Andy from the boob tube. Clay glared at the clock and waited for halftime. The screen claimed that was only three minutes away, but in football that could easily mean ten.

Twenty minutes later Andy lurched out of his chair with a grin. "I'll make some popcorn. You want another beer?"

"No, but thanks."

"How's the kid?"

"Annoying." Clay always had to fight to keep the pride out of his voice. "I sat down to help him with his homework tonight, and he's already ahead of me in math." Stalled in the doorway, Clay watched his oldest friend measure oil in a deep pan and set the burner on high. Andy was one of the few people on earth who'd let him ramble on and on about Spence, but for once his son wasn't on Clay's mind. "You know what I see a lot of in the bar?" he asked casually.

"Yeah. Good-looking single women."

"Newly divorced women," Clay corrected impatiently. When the first kernel popped, he moved by old habit to the refrigerator for the butter. "I see the same thing, over and over again. I don't care how old they are or how long they were married or what the story was. They all seem to go through the same stages to get through the divorce. First, there's the raw wound like grief. Maybe it is grief, for a marriage that died."

Andy shot him a look of mixed patience and humor. The man-to-man friendship had never been colored with philosophical discussions before, but he reasoned that old friends were occasionally entitled to brief spurts of insanity. Clay continued doggedly, "After that comes this panic stage. They're not sure they can cope alone, their confidence is gone, they're afraid of making a second mistake, of trying again...."

"You're feeling all right?" Andy interrupted.

"I'm feeling fine." Clay cleared his throat. "Anyway, those two stages are pretty tough on a woman, but the third stage is the most dangerous. Suddenly, the lady's euphoric. Freedom can be a pretty heady drug after being tied down with problems for a long time. So she's suddenly in a hurry to break out, prove she's still attractive, that there's fun to be had out of life again. And that's fine ... except that I see a lot of women do things they wouldn't normally do, make changes too fast, act out of character, maybe even go a little, well, wild."

"Very interesting," Andy said gravely.

Clay raked a hand through his hair. "Look, I'm trying to talk to you about Liz."

"My *sister*?" Andy shook his head with a laugh. "Come on, Clay. You know Liz as well as I do. I'm not saying she didn't take it hard and she's had this idiotic idea it was all her fault. Still, she's got a good head on her shoulders and always has had."

"Yes."

"Liz is as stable as apple pie."

"Yes."

"She just isn't the type to go wild."

"Yes," Clay agreed again, and thought "no" to all of the above. He should have known that talking to Andy was useless. Liz would never let her brother see anything but a fast-moving lady with bright eyes and a gift for laughter.

Dallas played a running game until past eleven o'clock. The popcorn bowl was empty and Liz still wasn't home. Clay nursed a beer until the fizz died, checked the clock approximately every three seconds and tried to talk himself out of a nagging case of rest-lessness.

He'd avoided her for a week. Liz's problems were none of his business, and exposure to Liz had always had the danger of dynamite to him. A classy lady with a summa cum laude degree didn't need a man with a past anywhere near her. Heck, he'd barely graduated from high school although he'd seen a lot of life.

He couldn't stop thinking about how blithely she'd talked about giving up her career, moving, changing her whole life.

He couldn't stop thinking about how wildly, des-perately a little alcohol had loosened the vulnerable side of Liz.

She was at the breakout stage in a divorce. He knew it. He'd seen it a hundred times. From pain to scab to scar, it took certain stages to heal a wound and no one escaped those stages. That was fine. That was life. Only he didn't want Liz hurt.

"What the heck has gotten into you this evening?" Andy demanded finally. "You didn't even notice the last touchdown."

"Sure I did." He hadn't. When the front door-knob clicked, he popped out of the chair as if he were struck by lightning, ignoring his old friend's stare.

She was slipping off her jacket as she suddenly stopped in the doorway. He saw first that she wore no lipstick—or maybe she had, and a man's mouth had rubbed it off. His nerves moved past edgy and into brittle. She was dressed in a pink angora sweater that showed off her breasts. The skirt advertised too much leg. Her cheeks had the kiss of cold air—and if she'd come straight home from a movie, she would have been nice and pale.

"Where have you been?" The words snapped out before he could stop them.

Liz finished peeling off her jacket, arching an eyebrow for the question. If she hadn't expected Clay, the blood had started zooming through her veins the instant she saw his car in the drive.

Seeing his son that afternoon had produced a chain of demands in her mind. Demands from the heart that she face up to what she really felt for Clay, what she'd always felt, and why. Wanting him had colored her life.

And at a single glance she knew ruefully that it still did. Even when he was glowering at her, Clay sent her heart thumping. He was dressed in jeans and a ragged sweatshirt. She wished he were naked.

Prim, stable librarians weren't supposed to think things like that. This quest for emotional honesty was like opening Pandora's box. Just feel, Liz, a voice inside her head chided. Well, that *sounded* georgy peachy. It was also scary as hell. Scary, upsetting, unnerving and perhaps just a little fun.

"Out," she answered his question wryly, and moved toward the popcorn bowl with a glare for her brother. "How could you?"

"Clay ate half of it."

"You both belong in a sty. You could have saved a little. Dallas survive without me?"

"No," Andy said glumly.

"Out with anyone I know?" Clay managed to lower his voice from caveman boom to civilized casual. It still earned him a wisp of a grin from Liz.

"Frank Butler. You remember him, don't you? I went to the senior prom with him. I gather since then he's been married, divorced and took over his dad's hardware store."

And frequented Clay's bar far too many Friday nights. Clay's glower darkened. He found himself trailing Liz to the hall closet, where she hung up her jacket, to the kitchen, where she deposited the popcorn bowl, to the doorway, where she suddenly stood with hands on hips, radiating patience. "Okay if I go to the bathroom alone?" she asked lightly.

He was waiting for her when she came out. "I wasn't following you."

"I could see that."

"You tired, or you got a few minutes to talk?"

She hesitated. "Andy?" After telling her brother they'd be out, she grabbed her coat, unsure what she was letting herself in for. A prowling tiger would have been easier to handle. Clay's mouth was in a thin line, his shoulders tense, and his eyes dared anyone to cross him.

She tiptoed with him out to the long wooden swing with the rusty metal chains. It seemed a good location to soothe a tiger. Leaves were drifting down from the maple tree. The autumn sky was peppered with stars. The air was soul-renewing cold and the night as soft as black silk. "How can anyone not love the fall?" she asked idly.

Clay didn't seem impressed. She curled up on one end of the swing with her knees tucked under her chin, he sprawled at the opposite end with one foot on the ground to keep the swing in motion. Their positions were the ones they'd used ten years before. The leather jacket he wore was as old as as the first time they'd ever sat that way. Silence washed over both of them. She figured he needed it.

She watched the play of moonlight on his face. In some ways, ten years of hard living showed in tucks and crinkles and lines. In other ways, he hadn't changed at all. The chip on his shoulder was still there, just better hidden. Defiance, strength, challenge—he didn't parade them around anymore, but the old toughness was still his first defense.

The night, the swinging rhythm and the darkness gradually worked its magic. She could see the frown easing from his features and had the oddest urge to hold him. It wasn't sexual, but he'd known so little love in his life and had fought for everything he had.

"Rough day?" she asked finally.

"Hectic." He leaned back, stretching his arms behind his head. "Which you must have guessed. I guess I came off a little abrupt in there."

"Slightly," she said dryly. The swing chains creaked in a rhythmic whisper.

"You have a good time with Frank?"

"Yes."

"Going out with him again?"

"No." All it took to make the man relax was to give him what he wanted. "It's been fun to be home, look up the old crowd I went to school with. Frank was always good company—he's got a terrific sense of humor. He hasn't changed much, though. He was always a surface man, if you know what I mean?"

"Yes."

"I could kick you," she said conversationally.

His eyes raised in surprise, shaded by moonlight.

"Could you try and believe I'm capable of judging a man's character all by myself, would you? You think I'm still seventeen?"

"I think," Clay said slowly, "that you are far more special, far more beautiful, far more dangerous than you came even close to being at seventeen."

She smiled. "Was that supposed to be a compliment or an insult?"

"You don't seriously expect me to answer that question."

She chuckled, resting her head against the back of the swing. The chains creaked and pulled, creaked and pulled. The privacy of darkness soothed like perfume, cool, sweet-scented, soft. "Clay?" Her eyes pierced his in the darkness.

"Hmm?" He'd forgotten how quiet she was. How she could take a tumble-fast noisy frantic world and turn the whole thing down when he was near her.

Her voice was husky, low. "I don't want you worrying about me. I've hit a rough patch; I've made some mistakes I'm having a tough time living with. That's not to say I can't handle my life. I didn't come home because I thought it would be easier here, but because I needed a place to come to terms. I have to do that alone."

He was silent for a moment, and then in one swift motion reached forward and twisted her around. Liz didn't argue, but it was more than a surprise to suddenly find her back cradled to his chest, his chin locked on the crown of her head and his arms laced around her stomach. "Now you listen, sunshine. I've made more mistakes in a day than you could make in an entire lifetime. You need someone to talk to, I'm here, and don't you ever forget it. Everyone needs help sometimes."

The scold was intended as comfort, she knew, just as the hug was intended as nothing more than to give her someone to hold on to. Unfortunately, a simple cuddle between leather and down jackets, jeans and sweaters, and she could feel a slow sweet ache spread from her fingertips to her toes. The cold October night abruptly turned sultry.

"Did you hear me?"

She tilted her head back. "Yes. Everyone needs someone. So when do you, Clay?"

He raised his eyebrows. "Feeling lonely and scared comes with life. I never said I was immune. I'm just saying I've been around the block a few times more than you have. Being too proud to call out for help when you need it is nonsense."

She persisted. "So when have you ever asked for help from anyone?"

"Liz..."

He was trying to shift, and was getting irritable. She felt a mix of old impatience and new determination; they both surprised her with their power. Clay had always offered her comfort, strength, trust. But the terms of that unequal friendship had always been his. She wasn't supposed to offer him the same things back. She wasn't supposed to feel the imprint of his thigh and manhood through layers of clothes, or experience firecracker sparks wherever flesh touched flesh.

But she did. It seemed past time to announce to Clay that she wasn't a toddler, but a woman who knew loneliness—as he did. A woman who knew pain and mistakes—as he did. She'd had nothing to give him as a teenager. On the surface she had less to offer him now, with her life in transition, but that wasn't wholly true. She knew more of men and more of life, enough to recognize a man who gave without taking, a man who'd given to her for eons without ever asking for anything back. So softly, she said, "Two can play this scolding game, you know. You think you've been around so much?"

"I know I have."

"Too much wine, women and song?"

"There's no way to have too much of any of those."

She shook her head, twisting so she could see his face. "I don't think so. I don't think you've had nearly enough—of fun, of laughter, of people in your life you could trust. Of women in your life who've gotten under the surface."

His lips opened with a flip reply that was never said. Silence happened the instant she touched his cheek. Her fingertips were cold on his warm skin. Her thumb traced the strong bone of his jaw and, the bristle of beard. Above the thin line of his mouth, his eyes glinted at her, impatient and black. At the first contact of her hand, the Adam's apple in his throat took on a steady pulse all on its own. Clay would have the whole world believe he was invulnerable, but Liz knew it wasn't true.

When he finally spoke, his tone was lazy and quiet, amused. "What do you think you're doing?"

Her eyes met his. It was perfectly obvious what she was doing.

Her fingers threaded in his hair. The texture was thick and clean, but not soft. Nothing about Clay was soft. In fact, he was suddenly as tense as the twisted cloud before a tornado. His hand abruptly clamped over hers. "The lady's old enough to have more sense than to bait the bear."

"Yes," she agreed calmly.

"Did Butler ply you with a little wine after the movie?"

"Not a drop." Softer than a butterfly, she pressed her lips to his. He didn't move. As far as she could tell, he stopped breathing. A statue could have been more responsive. Like a parent with an errant toddler, he'd evidently decided to wait out her bad behavior until she came to her senses.

It was a mistake on his part, because she was already coming to her senses by celebrating touch and smell and taste. Celebrating terrifying emotions that for years she'd tried to pretend weren't there. They were there, and if desire for Clay had colored her life, she had to know if she had ever colored his.

"Liz—"

She heard the vibration of last-straw impatience in his voice. She felt his hands tense on her shoulders and knew he intended to sever the contact. But he didn't. Foolish man, his mouth suddenly descended on hers when she wasn't going anywhere.

Her lips parted willingly, absorbing the pressure, tasting the flavor of him. She'd been wrong. One part of Clay was incomparably soft, vulnerable. His mouth offered an explosion of hunger, fierce and sweet. He suddenly molded her to him as if he were missing part of himself. Unsteady fingertips touched her face, dragged through her hair, anchoring her still for kiss after kiss that he couldn't seem to stop. She didn't try.

There wasn't room on the swing for real lovemaking. She could feel the brace of his knee in her back, and one of her legs was awkwardly bent to his chest. It didn't matter. His tongue filled her mouth at the same time a raw, breaking sound came from deep in his throat.

She arched closer to him, feeling the pure, sharp physical need to be taken. The need was delicious and intensely powerful, yet the more minor of emotions flooding through her. No man had ever made her feel this needed, this wanted, this...whole. The rub of his mouth, the harsh beat of his heart, the rasp of his breath—Clay wasn't kissing anyone's kid sister.

His palm slid up her stockinged leg, claiming calf and then thigh. She claimed the cords of his neck, fingertips impatiently trying to find skin under jacket and shirt. The zipper on her jacket rasped down in the silent night. His palm found her breast, throat and more thigh. Her body parts disassembled into those that were heavy and hot and those he hadn't touched yet. He seemed in a fierce angry hurry to touch everything all at once, to claim, protect, cover, discover. To know. Intimately. Now.

A single leaf created the interruption. Just one drifted down from the maple, red and crisp, landing on his shoulder. He reared back as if he'd been struck with a brick. His dark eyes exhibited just that amount of pain, and a man late to catch a train couldn't have shown more stress. He stood her up with him, arranged her skirt, her sweater, zipped her jacket as high as she'd need it for a blizzard.

She watched the moonlight play light and shadow on his frown and the set line of his jaw. Her knees wanted to cross. They could probably have heard his breathing in Milwaukee.

"Now listen," he said darkly.

But then he didn't say anything. He just placed his hands on his hips and then dragged them through his hair. He glanced at the sky and then at her shoulder, but they both avoided each others' gazes like the repel of two positive magnets. Finally he tried talking again. "Look, that was an accident."

"Yes."

"You always trusted me. I won't break that trust, Liz. It won't happen again."

"I have always trusted you and I trust you now," she agreed, "but I think, very definitely, that this is going to happen again."

"No, it isn't."

With the exact same proprietorial gestures, she reached up, straightened his shirt, zipped up his jacket, matched his glowering frown. Guardians did such things. Guardians of the heart.

At his exasperated sigh, she looked up. He wasn't any less tense, but an unwilling spark of humor was trying to tease his mouth into softening. "You're going to be trouble, aren't you?" he said dryly.

"Yes. Now have we got that settled?"

"*Liz.*"

She shook her head, her throat still thick with desire, the ache of need, a fierce exultation that he'd

wanted her, a troubling despair that he obviously
didn't want to admit it.

She touched his cheek, and walked to the door.

# Four

Two nights later Liz was counting sheep at two in the morning—and camels, llamas and yaks. None of them was denting her insomnia, which was why she so instantly recognized the difference between the cold patter of rain to the patter of small pebbles on her window.

The man standing on the lawn at ground level looked wet, cold and impatient. The fool was only wearing a leather jacket, and his fox-blond hair had a wet sheen like a pelt. Shaking her head she pulled on jeans, socks and a turtleneck, and then stumbled through the dark hall down the stairs.

As fast as she opened the front door, Clay stepped

in. Again, she shook her head sleepily. "I'm out of straitjackets. Pity."

"You look wide awake, so no excuses. You need boots, scarf, a jacket and gloves."

"It's raining. Didn't anyone mention it to you? Winter rain, not summer rain. We're talking as cold as sleet."

"I've been out in it. I know." He ducked behind the closet door in the front hall, passed her a jacket and a scarf. "Where's your boots?"

"Where's your head? Do you know what time it is?"

"Two going on three." He handed her gloves, one white, one red.

"You actually tell time," Liz said admiringly. A stocking cap muffled her next comment. Like a puppet, she felt her arms being fitted into the jacket sleeves. She handled her own boots and gloves, keeping a wary eye on Clay at the same time.

He'd never specialized in predictability, but he seemed extraordinarily hard to read at the moment. His face was washed with cold rain, even his cheeks and eyelashes were wet. He was moving with his usual lazy assurance, but his eyes had the snap and bleakness of a man going off to war.

"You want someone to share a case of pneumonia with?" she tried guessing.

"Nobody catches cold walking in the rain, or you wouldn't be going," he assured her.

Outside, she had only to leave the doorstep to feel every muscle instantly freeze. The rain felt like big fat drops of ice. Not a single light was on in the neighborhood. The street looked like a black shining skating rink. "So where are we going at this time of night?" she tried again.

"We're taking Trouble for a walk."

"Aaah. Who would have guessed that a few kisses on a backyard swing would upset a big, strong man like you?"

He nudged her into the walking pace of an Olympic trainer. "The day kisses from a half-pint blonde shake me, I'll let you know. This walk isn't for me. It's for you."

"Oh?"

"Ever walked in the rain before?"

She thought, then admitted, "No."

"Good. You were talking wanting to do things you never did before. Besides, you need exercise."

Because exhausted women were less likely to cause a man trouble? She shot Clay an amused glance.

She fell silent as they walked block after block. He was right that she'd never walked in the rain. Rain was an annoyance, something that affected a woman's choice of apparel to and from her way to work. She'd never considered enjoying it. She'd never considered breathing it, smelling it, tasting it.

Her tongue flicked out for a taste, and she heard Clay's chuckle. There was no doubt in her mind that if he had another woman alone at two o'clock in the morning, he wouldn't be freezing his toes on a rain-drenching walk. But she'd never wanted to be part of a herd, and whether or not Clay knew it, he was relaxing. His stride loosened, he threw his head back. His eyes took on a mischievous glint when he saw her smiling.

They didn't talk. They walked until her legs ached, until sleepiness and the dark wet rain and silence folded her in a sensual envelope. Life was so good. With Clay, she felt something new, a new strength and glow building inside her. What seemed natural with Clay had never been natural for her with another man.

It was nearing dawn when they returned to her house. "You'll sleep now," he told her, though he couldn't possibly have known how troubled her sleep had been for the past few nights.

"Clay?"

He was walking toward his car, but turned back. His face had the ruddy clean wash of the rain; his brows were matted with dampness. All she could think of was that he'd given her something again, free and clear, with no fanfare and no flag waving. "Thanks," she whispered. Then, on impulse, she reached up and pressed her lips to his.

He claimed the kisses of a half-pint blonde didn't shake him, but she felt the fast shudder that rippled through him, tasted yearning under the lingering crush of his mouth, saw his eyes close tight.

When he stepped back, he sighed, hard. "No." It seemed to cover everything he wanted to say, but she was still standing there when he reached his car. He folded both arms on the top of the car hood for a minute, as if mentally debating something, and then said, "You said you wanted to meet my son, and Halloween's just a few days around the corner. Six-thirty?''

At seven o'clock on Halloween, Clay discovered that his shoulder was glued to the bathroom doorway. A few nights before, it had seemed a good idea for Liz to meet Spence.

The walk in the rain had been designed to take Liz's mind off her fresh divorce. Clay hadn't stopped worrying about her since the night on her backyard swing. Liz was a dangerously vulnerable woman. Like anyone going through a rough patch, she needed comfort, someone to hold and listen, and what had driven him darn well nuts was knowing another man could have been on that backyard swing with her. Another man who would have taken advantage of her alluring beauty, her giving nature, the magical draw of her sensuality.

Liz very obviously needed to be steered away from backyard swings. A walk in the rain—all that nice exercise, all those nice wet, dripping cold conditions—had seemed a great option. Nobody thought of desire when they were sopping.

Except that Clay had. Obsessively. When she'd tilted her rain-wet mouth to his, all he could think about was a woman's skin beneath his hands, a woman's lips hot and willing beneath his, a woman's eyes intimately dark with need and promise.

He wasn't going to desert Liz in a time of trouble, but he intended to make certain any further circumstances for physical closeness didn't exist. Halloween had seemed perfect. She'd wanted to meet his son, and Clay's conscience was sort of clear.

Not that Spence didn't like girls, but Clay's son never talked to a female if a dog was in the same room. When it came down to it, for years, Spence had made a regular habit of terrorizing any woman who came near his life. Not that Clay wanted to put Liz through an ordeal, but when a man had an in-house chaperon of that magnitude... An evening trick-or-treating with Spence would keep Liz busy. It would also keep Clay's mind off dangerous inclinations where his sunshine was concerned.

Except that he hadn't quite anticipated Liz's showing up at the door dressed in a tattered calico skirt, with fake freckles dotting her nose and straggly braids tucked behind her ears. Neither, obviously, had his son.

"More gruesome, please." Spence's demand brought Clay out of his reverie.

"You don't think you look gruesome enough?"

"Heck, no. I want to look terrifying. Awesome. Blood-dripping scary."

"Can do, sweetie." Liz bent over Clay's son with a small white tube. Spence was sitting on the toilet seat, his legs crossed and his face tilted up. His face was your basic white, with one square blue eye and both eyebrows painted a screaming yellow. Slowly but surely she dribbled a streak of red down the side of his mouth, then stepped back to study his face.

"Now look," she suggested.

Spence jumped up with one tennis shoe perched on the toilet seat so he could tilt his head in the mirror. "Hell, I look wonderful!"

"Don't swear." They were the first words Clay had managed to squeeze in for the past half hour.

The ghoul ignored him, but the waif with the soft brown eyes shot him another curious look that said, I thought you told me he didn't like women.

What could he say? Spence hadn't shut up from the instant she'd walked in with the tube of fake blood and the makeup kit.

"You think I need a little more blood?"

Liz gave Spence another critical glance. "I think you look just fine. On the other hand, a guy can't have too much blood on Halloween. It's up to you."

"What do you think, Dad?"

"I think it's time we took you two—" Clay cleared his throat "—children on the road if you expect to fill up those trick-or-treat bags."

Where Clay first stopped the car, the neighborhood block was lit up with porch and streetlights and pumpkins with flickering candles inside. Residents could have auditioned for a horror movie. The entire population had shrunk to a range of two to four feet. Clowns raced along with Draculas. Witches bobbed next to urchins with plastic masks. One live St. Bernard with a pail around his neck escorted his charges to each door. A bit of greed, fear and mischief scented the air.

The waif and the ghoul hit five houses before running, laughing, back to the car. Liz slammed in beside Clay with hip-bumping power. "Look at the loot!" she crowed.

"Yeah. Wanna trade?" Spence was filtering through his bag.

"Of course I want to trade. I hate jawbreakers. What have you got in the way of nuts?"

Clay's fingers kneaded the increasingly tight muscle at the back of his neck. "I didn't know you planned on going out there with him," he murmured sotto voce.

"I promised your son," Liz responded simply, which obviously settled the issue for her.

Issues for Clay were becoming slightly more confused. He was astounded but delighted that Liz and Spence were getting along, until the vagrant thought popped in his head that the three of them were having a dangerously good time and he realized that a man could become easily addicted to the blend of a boy and a woman's laughter.

It took two hours before the two were finally exhausted. Back in the motel parking lot, Clay took Spence to the door before escorting Liz back to her car. "You head in to Cameron to show him everything. I'll be there in two shakes."

"I never got this much stuff in my life. We have to take her again," Spence said feelingly. "She's wonderful, Dad."

Clay had already noticed that every time Liz "traded," her trick-or-treat bag became miraculously empty while his son's bulged to seam-splitting proportions. That odd muscle was pulling at his nape again. Rubbing it, he strode back toward the half-pint blonde with the freckles, who seemed to effortlessly charm the Stewart men.

She was leaning back against her car door, keys dangling in her hand. Her dancing eyes made him nervous. "What a terrific kid he is, Clay! And I think he paid me the ultimate compliment. He said I wasn't like a girl at all. He said I was—almost—like a regular person."

"How old do you think a kid has to be before he can learn a little tact?" Clay asked weakly.

She laughed and surged toward him. He would have sidestepped if there had been time, but her fingers quickly hooked loosely around his neck. "Thank you for asking me. I had an absolutely wonderful time." She popped up on tiptoe, and maybe she only intended a peck of a kiss.

Her lips tasted like candy canes and chocolate. They tasted like innocence and happiness and laughter, and Clay tried to keep the image of a freckle-faced waif in his head. He even tried thinking of the potential dental bills she'd accumulated for him by feeding his son that candy.

Dental bills couldn't compete with the scent of yellow roses. With a will of their own, his hands shifted to her hair, loosening her braids. She was so small, her body so fragile. Liz always tasted like something he'd never had, couldn't have, shouldn't want.

She could make a man forget . . . ugliness. The ugliness of growing up with the stigma of bastard. Ugly memories of a kitchen full more with his mother's empty bottles than with food. Memories of being turned down for part-time jobs as a kid because of who he was, of using his fists to get back at the world, of trying to do the right thing too damn many times and somehow always doing the wrong one.

He'd grown up for Spence, and fought to climb out of that emotional gutter. But every time he touched Liz the old stamp of loser haunted him. He wasn't a nice man; he wasn't a white knight. More than one woman had flung the epithet of "ruthless" in his face.

And Liz was so damn crazy. She kissed him as if she were kissing sunshine, vulnerable, open, giving. He reared back suddenly, and felt appalled when he looked at her. Her lips were red from the pressure he'd exerted on them. Her eyes sleepily glowed with sensuality; he'd completely messed up her hair.

"No," he said hoarsely.

"It's all right, Clay—"

"It isn't."

For once, just once in his life, he was going to do the right thing. A man who'd been down as many dark roads as he had didn't tamper with something precious to him. Not with a woman as precious and vulnerable as Liz.

For as long as Liz could remember the downstairs bathroom's faucet had leaked. Well aware that her cream wool skirt and apricot-colored blouse were unsuited to plumbing work, Liz fetched her father's old tool kit from the basement, pushed up her sleeves and bent determinedly over the sink anyway.

Andy had left for a Friday night date and the hall clock chimed six. An ideal time, as far as Liz was concerned, to fix an old problem.

She fussed with the faucet top and cap, but the set screw didn't want to give, surprising her not at all. So far this week, she hadn't found a single good fairy in residence. Every old problem she was determined to solve was stubbornly hanging in there, beginning with job hunting and ending with Clay.

She reached for the old container of penetrating oil, wishing she could apply a little of it directly to Clay Stewart's brain . . . before or after a wrench had been applied to his hard head. On second thought, neither would dent anything *that* unyielding.

Last week had been just like old times, with Clay spontaneously showing up on a regular basis. Monday after school he and Spence arrived, Spence with a dirt bike and Clay with a rented tandem cycle, insisting she join them for a ride to the river. He'd shown up on Tuesday with two boxes of sinfully rich chocolate éclairs—her vice. Wednesday he'd brought Spence and the three of them had raked leaves.

Every day there'd been something. Only every day his conversation had also been strewn with "sunshines" and "kiddos" and "short stuffs." He ruffled her hair as often as he did Spence's. He teased her for being out of shape. Liz wasn't blind and Clay didn't have to shout that he still saw her as an adopted sister.

So she was never going to appeal to him as a lover? Fine. Doubts about herself as a woman, guilt about her failed marriage added up fast. She was currently out of a job and had nothing but rootless, rotten credentials to apply to a relationship. She had no basis whatsoever to believe he cared for her.

Except that he shuddered whenever she touched him. Whenever she saw him with Spence, she saw a fiercely protective father who was far too sensitive about his background. The old Clay had the same bleak loneliness in his eyes as the new one, but he was still the kind of man who gave and gave, but had the hardest time taking back. Who was ever there for him?

If Liz were honest with herself, the man only had to be in the same city to make her personal earth move.

A few weeks ago she'd thought being honest with herself, believing in herself, trusting her instincts as a woman, and acting on her feelings were terribly important. Running was really a lot easier. She'd always been good at running. Outstanding, in fact.

Falling in love with the wrong man at the wrong time was very similar to jumping off a cliff. And jumping off a cliff wasn't any fun. Particularly when the man's favorite word was ''no'' and he made an annoying habit out of ruffling her hair.

The darned faucet refused to fix. The penetrating oil loosened the set screw, but as soon as Liz turned the wrench, water gushed like a miniature Old Faithful. She shot a fast scowl upwards that said, Thanks, I needed this. Twisting the wrench around double time, she heard a pounding on the back door.

"Just a minute!" she yelled out, and then jerked to her feet and reached for a rag—naturally there was no rag. Could one single thing go right this week? The water was still gushing, and the door pounding continued. Exasperated, she flew to the back door.

Through the casement panes, she saw Clay illuminated by the yellow yard light. His blond hair was whipped up in the wind and sculpted an ancient denim jacket to his chest. Another impromptu visit between old buddies, she thought helplessly.

He pushed open the door, bringing with him a surge of fresh cold air and a dominantly male grin. Her pulse had no sense; it picked up erratically. Heat annoyingly collected in the private parts of her body. Mercilessly subdued hormones burst to life, and all Clay was doing was laughing at the oily mess on her hands.

"Don't tell me what you're up to. I don't want to know."

"Plumbing," she confessed ruefully, and wished she could jam a cold hard lid on that entire box of honesty. The pulse, the heat and the hormones could get packed in with it.

"In trouble?" he quizzed.

"You don't know the half of it." Her smile was ironic, until she abruptly remembered she had no time for smiles. She rushed back to her flood, trailed by Clay, who took one look, crouched on his haunches and grabbed the wrench. The grin on his face spoke volumes. "Don't you dare say one word," she continued. "I know what needs fixing. It's just an O-ring, and it certainly doesn't take brawn to replace an O-ring."

"Ah. I recognize a women's lib crisis, but at the risk of having a stone aimed at my head—did you consider asking Andy to take this on?"

"My brother? Have you ever seen him change the oil in a car? You're talking seven hours of cuss words and grease from here to Milwaukee. Besides, I can't stand women who get heart palpitations at the sight of a hammer. I am perfectly capable...." She sighed. All he had had to do was turn the wrench and the water had stopped gushing.

Clay's tone dripped apologies. "Look. If you want, I'll loosen it all up again and you can fix it. I'll just stand there looking small and helpless and meek."

It was the image of a meek Clay that dissolved exasperation into laughter. She dropped a towel on his head and another two on the floor to clean up the puddle. "In the next life I'm going to have the shoulders of a linebacker and the grip of a wrestler," she informed him.

"At the risk of raining more trouble on my head, you'll look pretty silly if you keep those legs with your new body." He piled the tools back in the box. Seconds later they both leaned over the sink to wash their hands.

"Chauvinist," Liz muttered, still laughing, but she shot him a quick look. She *did* have nice legs but had never thought Clay had noticed. "Where's Spence?" she asked abruptly, head down over soap and water.

Their wet fingers touched. Clay's hands were huge next to her own, his flat squared nails a contrast to her curved ones, the beige hair on his knuckles distinctly different from her own slim white fingers. A man's hands. A woman's hands. Man. Woman. Sex. Why don't you send that overactive libido back to its cage, Elizabeth? she thought.

"He's spending the night at a friend's."

"Earning a little free time for you? Except obviously the opposite is true—Friday nights must be the busiest in your business."

"Always," Clay agreed. "I left a packed restaurant, an overbooked motel and an overflowing bar—seemed an excellent time to play hooky. Got a pair of high-heeled sneakers?" He handed her a towel.

"Pardon?"

"We're going dancing."

A mere twenty-seven and her hearing was going. She smiled at him. "For a minute I thought you said . . ."

"Where's your coat?"

She found her coat, and an hour and a half later, she found herself sitting in a velvet-cushioned chair at the club, trying to make sense of the gold-tipped hors d'oeuvres menu in her hand. Either the printing was in hieroglyphics or she'd completely forgotten how to read.

Thistles was halfway to Milwaukee and catered to the country club set: tuxedoed waiters, Irish linen, sterling and rosebud centerpieces, a three-piece combo cycling love songs from the past five decades. Liz peeked over the top of the menu again. Clay was still sitting across from her, his denim jacket tossed aside and his white shirt straining his broad shoulders. He looked all right. He looked like Clay.

Only Clay had always hated country clubs with their pretentiousness and formality. He had a terrific restaurant of his own if he was hungry, and over the weeks she'd been home he'd made clear that she was the last woman he associated with dinner and dancing.

Possibly he was ill.

His eyes met hers. He smiled. She smiled back. He had to be ill. Brain tumor?

A mild-eyed waiter suddenly hovered. "Mind if I choose?" Clay asked her. She shook her head. "A magnum of Château Lafitte for the lady..."

Her jaw dropped.

"And for you, sir?"

"Beer-whatever you have on draft. Liz, you want some kind of hors d'oeuvres?"

What she wanted was nitroglycerine for her impending heart attack. Her tongue refused to function for several seconds. "I'd like a side order of oysters, please," she finally told the waiter.

Clay's eyes flashed quick surprise, and her chin tilted at a reckless angle. All right, maybe she'd never tried oysters before, but it seemed time to stop dithering and go with the flow. She still couldn't fathom why he'd dragged her to this insanely overpriced, snobbish restaurant; he sure as heck wouldn't have taken his little sister here. But she was a female and of age, capable and accountable for taking an uninhibited risk here and there. As soon as the waiter was out of sight, she leaned over the table. "Quick! Call him back!"

"Who?"

"The waiter," she hissed frantically.

A wicked grin curved into his cheeks. "I thought you'd change your mind about those oysters—"

"Not for those, you nut. For the champagne. Didn't you see the price tag on that champagne? A hundred and fourteen dollars a bottle!"

"If you don't like it, you can pour it in the rose vase," he consoled her.

"That's not the point! Clay, it's crazy to waste good champagne on someone who barely drinks—"

"There should be time for at least one dance before he comes back with the goodies." He stood up and reached out a hand.

When they returned to the table, Clay's beer was sitting with a fine head of foam and the waiter was waiting to pour the champagne. Liz touched her fingers to her temples as she sat down. The combo had been playing a waltz. She hadn't danced an old-fashioned romantic waltz since she could remember, much less with an escort who had held her as if they were in a Viennese ballroom.

"So tell me about your job hunting. Having a rough time?"

"A little," she admitted.

"You checked with the library and school to see if they had openings for a librarian?"

For a moment she couldn't talk. Clay had taken up staring at her across the table, dark eyes flirting with her, intimately chasing down the movement of her lips, resting on her white throat, dawdling on the rise and fall of her breasts.

"No, I didn't check around for any potential librarian jobs," she said finally.

"Why, honey?"

She paused before answering while she took a sip of champagne. His told-you-so grin suggested that she found the sparkling drink worth a reverent moment of silence. It did, but her head was reeling far more from the heady, exotic rush caused by the way he looked at her.

"Liz?"

"I was going to answer you. It's simply hard to explain," she admitted honestly. "I worked hard for that librarian's degree, and on the surface it must look silly to throw it away and look for something else. For that matter, the job I had was secure and safe, stable." She hesitated when the waiter set the plate of oysters in front of her.

The little silvery-gray globs were served in the shell and attractively garnished with greenery. They looked...slippery. They looked like something only a brave, uninhibited woman would try. Clay's gaze riveted to her face, and she deliberately picked up the tiny sterling oyster fork. Maybe she imagined it, but his roguish tone suddenly turned softer than ever.

"You've had it with 'secure and stable,' have you?"

"I've had it with being afraid of taking a chance," she affirmed, and took another sip of the champagne, the oyster fork still in her hand. "I don't want it anymore—day after day of working with paper instead of people. No air, no sunshine, no challenge, no...risk. Life seen through a window." The oyster slid on her tongue and just sat there like wet slimy rubber.

His tone never changed tempo. "Spit it into the napkin, sunshine. No one's looking. I couldn't give a hoot if they were."

She raised the spotless white napkin to her lips and faked a delicate cough. Gone. Too aware of Clay's eyes on her, she immediately took a wantonly long sip of champagne and fussed with the fork. Finally she cupped her chin in her hands and met his gaze. "Darn," she whispered ruefully.

His chuckle was earthy-low and as sexy as a whisper.

"I wanted to like them. I just wanted to try something new, Clay."

"Yes, and that's exactly why I brought you here, Elizabeth Brady. So you could try oysters and get silly on champagne if you wanted to," he said quietly. Something changed in his eyes. The lover's gleam became muted. The expression on his face darkened. "You need fun, Liz. We all do, and maybe especially after life's handed us a blow. So maybe you're not quite ready to marry again, to even look for a serious relationship with the right kind of man. But going out to dinner, a little flirting, a little champagne, a little dancing—it's not only fun, it's the best cure I know to chase the blues." He added deliberately, "When there's no risk involved."

After so much champagne her throat was suddenly bone-dry.

"No one's going to hurt you if you're with me, Liz, and we both know there's no chance of a serious relationship between us."

He made it sound as if the idea were worth a mutual chuckle.

A Ming vase in an earthquake couldn't have felt more perishable or fragile than Liz suddenly did. She'd thought, hoped, and misunderstood, everything. He'd taken out an old friend. Not a woman. Clay simply didn't want to see her as a woman.

Maybe it was past time she stopped wearing her heart on her sleeve for a man who clearly didn't want her.

# Five

Clay's motel had a heated indoor pool. Unfortunately, there were usually people in it, which was why he maintained a membership at the local Y. Thursday nights at ten o'clock the Olympic-size pool was always empty, and his huge annual contribution insured the doors were kept open until eleven for him.

When he stepped out of the locker room, the smell of chlorine invaded his nostrils. Heat and the reflection of aqua-blue waters made the white walls appear to shimmer and gleam. The blend of silence, privacy and water immediately began the process of soothing his tight nerves—until he noticed the huge pink towel on the bench. He wasn't alone.

His gaze riveted to the lone swimmer doing laps in the pool. Even from the distance to the far end, he could see the swimmer was female. His first thought was that only a man could have invented tank suits. His second, that he would have recognized that tight, tiny fanny anywhere.

He dropped his towel on the bench and watched from the pool's edge. She did three laps, then four. Heaven knew how many she'd finished before he walked in. Water and lady were one sensual part of each other. Both, he thought fleetingly, were something a man could drown in. Her kick barely stirred a froth of water and her crawl was graceful, but the pace she set was punishing. His eyes narrowed when she reached lap number ten.

The swimmer paused at the far end, breathing hard and painfully. Her hair was coiled in a single gold strand streaming down her back; droplets of water shimmered on her slim shoulders. He knew exhaustion when he saw it. She rested her head in her arms for a second and he thought, Damn you to hell, Liz. Get out.

She didn't. She pushed off with a slim foot, the backstroke this time. At his end, she switched to the crawl. Another lap. Another. The water licked at her body, fighting her.

Another lap, and she reached his side, gasping, her eyes blind from water, the pain in her lungs something he felt in his own. He had the pink towel ready.

"Out. Try poisoning your enemies, sunshine. You can't kill water. I've tried."

Liz's head jerked up in shock. The man at the desk had all but promised her no one used the pool on Thursday nights, only that it was open until eleven at night. She barely caught a glimpse of a too-bare Clay before his fingers closed around her arms, hauling her up.

She might have protested if she'd had the strength. Her lungs were self-righteously trying to collapse. All four limbs were weighted with fatigue. She'd pushed herself, then pushed some more until there was no energy left.

As fast as her rear end collided with the cement side, the pink towel was wrapped around her. The towel was giant size; it wrapped around twice. It occurred to her that she specifically didn't want to see Clay when she looked like a wet rat with blue lips, but vanity had to wait. Her lungs were both hauling in air and singing victory hymns. We don't have to swim anymore? Thank you, Liz.

In time she had additional breath. Once she wiped the moisture from her eyes, she let her eyes whisk over him. He was settled next to her, his legs in the water. He might as well have been naked. His cutoffs wouldn't have passed for decent on even a European beach. His chest was smooth and as solid as a wall, and his shoulders showed off physical power. No woman needed to be subjected to that when she could barely breathe.

The face should have been safer territory than the body, except that his eyes were waiting for that contact. Brown could be a dauntingly intimate color. She looked away.

"Alive yet?"

"Getting there." Dribbles of water still sneaked down her forehead. Irritated, she batted at them with the towel. "How's Spence?"

"On an immediate basis, fine, naturally—he's sleeping. On a more long-term basis, I seem to be raising a child who terrifies me. He's an eight-year-old tyrant, and he's smarter than I ever was. Nobody tells that monster what to do, and once he's decided he wants something, anybody standing in his way..." Clay shook his head.

"Take after anyone you know?" Liz asked dryly.

"Not me. The kid's a brain. I barely earned a high school diploma. The kid collects things. I never did. Spence has never been in trouble, any kind of trouble."

"Umm," Liz murmured, which seemed more tactful than mentioning Spence was his spitting image. Stubborn, willful and independent. The son had more ability to work within the system than the father. Beyond that, their differences were negligible. She was amazed Clay couldn't see it.

"Liz?"

She tilted her head.

"You've been avoiding me for a week. Never there when I call. Never around when I stop by."

"Avoiding you. Of course not. I've just been busy." A blatant lie, she thought fleetingly, and tugged the towel more closely around her body. She'd sworn to tell no more lies, not to anyone else and never to herself again. Only she was beginning to discover that honesty and self-preservation didn't necessarily go together.

The endless laps had been for Clay and, a little, for his son. As far as Spence was concerned, she adored the urchin and he'd seemed to take to her like butter on toast. It simply wasn't the right thing to do—spend too much time with the little one, let a relationship develop where a child might unconsciously build up expectations of permanence. Spence craved a mom, whether or not Clay knew it. And at Thistles, Clay had made more than clear that he wasn't looking for moms—or lovers. At least, not with Liz.

For the past week, she'd been celebrating exactly what she had—a friend. Friends tried oysters together. A certain breed of friend could be the most precious thing on earth—the kind one could talk to, share with, be oneself with, and know that no judgments would be made.

Clay motioned toward the water. "Were you mad at anyone I know?"

Just me, a little voice nagged at her. Because I darn well don't want to be friends with you, Clay. "I wasn't mad at anyone, just trying to exercise. I'm out of shape—"

"No, you're not, and you weren't just exercising."

She sighed irritably. "You came here to swim, didn't you? Well, swim."

With an inscrutable expression, Clay lurched to his feet and stalked to the far wall by the shower rooms.

He'd come here to swim, all right. Long hard laps that would keep a brown-eyed angel off his mind. That option had disappeared the moment he'd spotted Liz.

She was about to have a few options of her own disappear. Action always settled easier in Clay than thinking, and he'd done enough thinking about Liz over the past few days to cause him an ulcer.

The side of his palm hit the row of light switches. Blue waters immediately turned black. Moonlight barely peeked through the tall windows on the south wall.

"Clay? What on earth are you doing—"

"Remember how to play keep-away? Slip in the water, Liz. You'll be warmer."

"You play keep-away with a basketball, idiot. Turn on the lights!"

He couldn't. For a week of black nights, he'd pictured her face when they were talking in the restaurant. Until then maybe he'd guessed that her casually thrown kisses were not so casual, but that was exactly why he'd taken her to Thistles. It was exactly the kind of place where she belonged and he never would. His denim to her silk, his beer to her champagne, a waltz for a lady next to his rock 'n' rhythms bar. He'd thought she'd see what had always been obvious to him.

Only the look on her face bothered him. He'd never meant to hurt her, only to protect her. She needed someone, he knew that, and that any kind of rejection could be a particularly sensitive subject for a woman fresh from a divorce.

He'd spent a week well aware she was avoiding him, knowing how easily she could find another man to try oysters with, someone more than willing to hold a lady who desperately needed to be held. He'd spent a week knowing that he'd always specialized in doing the wrong things with the people close to him. He'd never helped his alcoholic mother. Mary couldn't imagine marriage to him even when she was pregnant. And his son, his Spence, had spent two years locked in a foster home because his father had a reputation for irresponsibility.

He didn't want Liz anywhere near him.

The twist that kept haunting him all week was that she was a terribly dangerous woman on a backyard swing. He'd come to the inalterable conclusion that the only man he trusted that close to her... was him.

"Take off your suit, skinny. This is a grown-up game."

He heard her indrawn breath, then an exasperated "I think you're nuts."

Clay had been called worse. The look in her eyes tore at his heart. She was doing a passably good job of eating herself up inside. The lady needed laughter, and he needed to hear her laughter.

"I'll give you to the count of ten and then I'm coming after you," he announced.

Liz tried to think through the count of three and then simply tossed off her towel and slipped into the water. Her head reeled off any number of denigrating epithets for Clay Stewart, most of which involved his demise.

The blackness enfolded her like a hollow dark cave. Her senses felt the prick of life and an incorrigible spirit of fun sneaked up on her. Keep-away from Clay struck her as the most humorous game in town. She'd been trying to do it half her life.

The water felt like warm silk as she glided soundlessly through the shallow end. She heard the splash when Clay dived in the pool, then instantly slid under the surface. When she emerged she was beneath the diving board and waited, breathless, eyes skimming the darkness for any sign of a shadow, ears alert to hear any noise.

Nothing except the soft drone of the filter, the smell of chlorine, the soothing lap of water and a cave of charcoal-black darkness. No splashes, no man shadows. Then from nowhere she felt an intimate pinch on her fanny. Her jaw dropped in shock and promptly filled with water. She came up sputtering and with a red face no one could see.

"Nice." The voice was as husky as mischief, drawling from the other side of the pool. "But you had your suit on. That's no fun, sunshine. You've got another count of ten to get it off—or I'll take it off for you."

"The heck you wi—" She started to say it, but alarm and laughter pulsed through her when she heard the splash. He aimed for the sound of her voice. Days of nervousness dissolved helplessly, not by choice but simply by what happened. She moved fast. For the pinch on her fanny, he deserved retribution.

"Now, honey. If you'll stay in one place you'll make this so much easier."

She dived underwater and held her breath, listening beneath the surface where all the sounds were magnified. He was treading water on the side. She swam closer, closer, soundlessly. The biggest lug on earth was weightless underwater. One strong wrench of his ankle and he went down. She escaped with all due speed.

"Oh, Liz. That was a terrible tactical mistake. Now you'll have to pay."

A hound couldn't have sounded more mournful. She grinned. For three and a half seconds she felt safe. From the center of the pool, she could escape in all four directions.

"Come on, darlin'. Take your punishment like a woman."

His arms were out, lapping the water, no longer trying to be quiet—undoubtedly a measure of the confidence he felt. Arrogance, Liz corrected wryly. But suddenly he made no sound. Adrenaline pumped in her veins; she barely breathed.

For an instant, she thought it was air on her shoulders. That fast, the shoulder straps of her suit slid down. For a second her arms were pinned. She felt the brush of bare male thigh and hand. Her whole body snapped on like a light switch.

He was right. This was an adult game, and one with a unique set of dangers when played with Clay.

She kicked off fast, her instinct to avoid his hands, his touch—yet no hands moved to stop her. She misunderstood that he was letting her free. He was letting her free, but in fact, he was using all the force of her fierce forward momentum to his advantage. He simply maintained a grasp of her suit straps and pulled down. The suit caught and pulled and netted once on her ankles, but then he had it. She was bare as a baby in the darkness.

From the shallow end, she heard a wicked "You know, Liz, from a man's point of view probably the only thing on earth more interesting than a woman in a tank suit is a woman without one."

Liz wasn't inclined toward obscene gestures, but there was a time and place. He'd never know any of her fingers were sticking up over the water anyway. So fast, though, she felt the sexy brush of a thumb on her bare nipples. Faster yet, the glide of a hand down her spine, down over her hip and thigh....

She burst from the water at the far end. Her heart wasn't beating; it was tingling. There was a devil somewhere in the darkness. A devil who'd changed rules on her. Clay had never initiated physical contact beyond a casual hug. It had always been her.

"Okay. Had enough? You're probably getting cold."

"I'm not cold."

"Tired then."

She understood from his brisk change in tone that he was trying to change the rules back. Now. Quickly. "We can't end the game without a winner," she insisted.

"Winner?"

"So how about five minutes to claim a quick kiss, Clay? Assuming you can find me."

A moment's silence, and then a snapped warning. "You're on."

Clay no longer wanted to play the game, and knew there was no way to measure time in the darkness. When he'd initiated the play, he'd deliberately added the spice of nakedness. It seemed a way of communicating to Liz that his rejection had never meant that he found her less than a beautiful, sexy lady. Flirting could be a confidence builder. A dash of wicked could send sluggish blood moving again. There had never been any harm because he knew it wasn't going too far.

He still knew it wasn't going too far, but he wanted the game over now, the lights on and the lady clothed. The water was dark as ink, the air heavy, and good intentions were trying to disintegrate into images of a smooth naked body blending with water and night. Liz's body. Liz's laughter.

Clay pushed off from the side, knowing exactly how quick that "quick kiss" was going to be when he found her. Emerging in the shallow end, he stilled when he heard the almost imperceptible whisper of her breathing. She was standing still as a statue three feet from him, then two. Her eyes gave her away.

From her eyes he knew where her mouth was. She couldn't know how carefully he avoided bodily contact. His lips touched hers, all he wanted and all he knew was going to happen, but every muscle in his body jammed tight. Her mouth yielded under his, slippery and warm. Don't do that, Liz, he silently cried out.

Her throat arched back with a virgin's trust. Dammit, don't do that, either. The choice for him to instantly pull back was there. He couldn't. For an instant he let knowledge flow through like torture. So close. Five inches closer and her small breasts could have nestled to his chest, all bare, all wet, all warm. In fantasies he'd protected her from a hundred dragons when he'd found her in darkness and danger.

They were in darkness now and she couldn't know how much danger she was in. With her, for her, he'd always wanted to be a hero. He knew all too well that he was incapable of being more than a man. The need to touch her clawed at him, and the sweet rub of her lips against his wasn't helping. Her fingers slid in his hair, everything dark, everything wet. Tongues.

Liz felt his fingers tighten on her shoulders. He didn't seem to know she'd have bruises for days. From the instant his mouth had touched hers, she'd felt the explosion of emotion in Clay. Blind in the dark, his lips had sought out her cheeks, her nose, her eyes, with kiss after kiss that cherished and branded. Such fierce hunger, such desperate loneliness. He kissed her like torment, like treasure. Did he even know what he was communicating to her?

Heat streaked up her veins and a wanton, delicious ache spread with powerful force through her body. Neither was the reason she stepped in, closed in, suddenly not Liz but Diana. The hunt was mythical; there was no prey, just a woman weary of pride and fibs. I'm sorry, Clay, but this one time I'm not going to believe you, but me. You want to play tease and tickle?

Only you shouldn't kiss that way if you don't want to play truth or consequences. Go ahead, love. Show me control, how much you don't need, how much you don't want, have never wanted me.

Water lapped between them, waist high, and then was displaced by the slide of wet skin on wet skin. At that first contact of breast and belly, Clay's throat released a low, short, angry sound, half groan, half growl. She trapped that sound with her mouth and felt the shudder that tracked through him.

His grip on her shoulders loosened. She paid no attention. The emotions reeling through her were pure, honest, powerful. His heartbeat was captured between her breasts. She slid her arms around him, tracing the ripples and slopes of his back, the taper of spine. Her lips touched his throat. She tasted water. She tasted Clay.

Her fingers raced, to touch, to arouse, to explore. To give. You need someone to give to you, Clay. Her lips glided over smooth wet skin, tender, swift. You need tenderness. Her breasts snuggled against him. And warmth. I don't care if you want it. I want it. I want you to know that there's someone there in the darkness.

His breath turned harsh. She heard his rasp of a scold, but that wasn't what his body communicated to her. Maybe reason had to disappear where there were no boundaries, nothing to hold on to but each other. His hands turned aching rough as they suddenly framed her face. His mouth came down with urgent pressure. His arousal pressed against her abdomen, heavy and hard. His chest layered against her small taut nipples until the water droplets between them were hot enough to make hot exotic tea.

Desire clutched in her stomach. The lure to back down was there. What exactly had she unleashed? Water and darkness, slick heat and a man coming apart with hunger, exploded with something nameless, desperate, dark, dangerous.

The fear dissolved magically. Suddenly, he wrapped her up and held on. She absorbed the giant shudder that racked his body, yielded for the hard drag of a last kiss and then he slowly pulled back. If she couldn't clearly see his face, she could see the sheen of his wet velvet eyes. "Possibly," he said lowly, "you're the most beautiful, dangerous woman I've ever known, sunshine."

"Yes?"

"I want you."

"Yes."

"I've always wanted you."

"Yes."

"Honey, unless you're in a mood to juggle any more dynamite, I'd advise you to quit saying yes."

She felt like laughing, and most of her bones had a lot in common with the collapsed spokes of an umbrella. Clay was edging her through the water to the pool side with dizzying speed, and then he lifted her up and was pushing the damp hair from her face with blind, smooth fingers.

"Could you stay out of trouble long enough for me to get the lights on? Don't answer that. Just stay put. I'll get your towel."

She had the towel wrapped around her before he snapped on the lights. A mystical fantasy of water and darkness abruptly turned into the Y. Her body announced she was both chilled and physically tired, when all she wanted to concentrate on was the sensual intimacy they'd just shared. A strong, stubborn man had finally admitted he'd wanted her, had always wanted her. She wanted to savor that. Instead, maybe due to the sudden harsh glare of bright lights, Clay now seemed someone else.

His hair was still dripping wet, but the low-slung derelict cutoffs were riding his lean hips again. For reasons she couldn't fathom he was striding the far side of the pool room checking doors. Putting distance between them. She couldn't care less what he was doing, and it wasn't the physical distance that disturbed her. Reality was just coming down with a bump, that was all. His eyes had a snapping alertness instead of warmth, his stride was arrogant again. Alluring soft words were no longer on his lips; instead she heard curses, one after another.

"What's wrong?" Draping the towel around her, she stood up, shivering suddenly.

Clay tested the last door. "We're locked in."

# Six

"We can't be locked in!"

"We are. Both shower doors, the main door to the pool..." Clay pushed back his wet hair. "My best guess is that someone discovered the lights were off and figured we'd gone home." He disappeared behind an open door.

Clutching the towel around her wet body, Liz followed him. The open door led to a pool closet, not too helpfully supplied with skimmers, vacuums and chlorine filters.

"I don't believe this." Clay stalked back out and past her, staring up at the one wall with windows. The windows were about nine feet up. They also looked locked.

Liz's gaze skimmed the room. Neither benches nor tile floors had much potential for a bed, and beyond her wet tank suit—now lying in a puddle on the floor—the towel was her only available covering. Both of their dry clothes were locked in the shower room. So was her purse and car keys...everything. "Have you any idea what time the Y opens in the morning?" she asked wryly.

"Honey, you won't care. You'll be home safe and snug in a bed."

"But how—"

"I've picked a lock or two in my time. I'll get you out— Don't put that on," he said abruptly, when he saw her picking up her wet tank suit. "Bare will be bad enough—it's colder than a stone outside—but bare and wet would be the same as begging for pneumonia."

Her eyes met his. Moments ago, bare with Clay had possessed some very special implications. Now his tone was so bland he could have been discussing the weather. Was he asking her to be a good girl and pretend it never happened?

"How are we leaving?" she asked politely.

"Through the windows."

"Did I miss seeing a pair of stilts in the pool closets? Come on, Clay. There's no way to reach those windows."

He flashed a lazy grin. "All my life, people have told me 'no way.' That's my favorite game in town."

No, she thought fleetingly, your favorite game in town is running hard and fast when people come too close.

Just like old times, a little trouble got him off the emotional hook. Obviously it wasn't the time to mull through his feelings or her own, but he didn't have to relish their situation. Any sane man would have felt a little stress at being locked in. Clay was enjoying it.

Liz told herself she wasn't really feeling hurt. Wet, cold, tired women had a right to feel irritable. Besides, his plan was bananas.

Clay had meanwhile found some kind of long-handled hook that unlocked the windows. Now he expected her to climb up to his shoulders, stand, and crawl out the narrow opening. Furthermore, he never asked her permission before hauling her up on his shoulders, and it was exactly then that she balked.

"Look, I can't."

"Yes, you can."

"I'm too heavy to stand on your shoulders. The window space is too small. It's too high—"

"The only reason you're dithering is because you think I'm going to see something. I've seen it all before, sunshine, and nobody's looking, anyway. Now come on."

Well, that was easy for him to say. He'd already tossed off her towel and the bump of bare breasts and fannies and awkward limbs had her heart pounding. She didn't have sex on her mind but when a woman's bare legs were wrapped around a man's neck, she was slightly inclined to distraction. Also wounded pride.

A half hour before he'd certainly seemed lovingly, exhilaratingly, passionately fascinated with her limbs. Now he seemed to regard them as nuisances.

"Even if I stand up on you—even if I make it through the window—I'll be afraid of falling on the other side."

"You're not going to fall."

"You willing to write up that guarantee?"

"Yes. What you're going to do, Liz, is wait at the top until I climb through the adjoining window; then I'll be outside and on the ground to catch you. Now come on." He patted her fanny impatiently.

She considered murdering him. Every fantasy she'd ever had of Clay Stewart involved bareness, but not like this. Not climbing up a wall with her bare feet on his shoulders, not with his having a bird's eye view of her rump when she awkwardly pulled herself up and grasped the window frame. Something hard and unyielding scraped her stomach en route.

The real insanity of the whole business didn't hit her until she was crouched unsteadily on the window frame, poised between a cold November night and a heated pool room, naked, her hair damp and straggly and her teeth chattering. Obviously, this wasn't happening. Heck, it wouldn't happen in a self-respecting nightmare.

With a panther's agility, Clay sprang from the bench, up through the window next to her, and then down. His grin was pure boyish. "I haven't had this much fun in ages. Let's go, short stuff." His hands beckoned the come-on.

Those hands were a long way down. The Y also hadn't spent a lot of money on landscaping. All she could see was frost-tipped grass and a big yellow autumn moon, not a tree or bush in sight. She took a breath and leaped.

He staggered against her weight, but the warm wrap of his arms never faltered. She saw something then— something fleeting and compellingly intimate in his dark eyes—and then it was gone. Her bare feet had had an instant to register shock at the prickly frosted grass before he'd grabbed her hand and was pulling her toward the two lone cars in the parking lot. All she could think of was that she was too old to be arrested for streaking.

"And your car keys, Clay," she gasped. "Weren't they locked in the shower room? And mine are in my purse. They're locked up, too."

She should have known Clay would be prepared for trouble. He had a spare car key taped under his car hood and a blanket—none too clean—folded up in his trunk. Seconds later, she was mummified in that oily smelling blanket, her knees tucked under her chin while Clay started the engine and heater.

He glanced at her. She was well aware what she looked like, from witch's hair to blue-cold lips to his stinky blanket to her protruding toes. Unaccountably her mouth started twitching.

His quick grin suddenly erupted into full-bodied, throw-back-his-head laughter. Suddenly, she was laughing, too.

"Only with you, sunshine," he murmured. "Only with you."

Her heart was ticking with a steady rhythm. With a simple three-word phrase he'd managed to get himself forgiven for all of his dictatorial behavior. When his laughter naturally faded the lazy grin stayed but his eyes were protruding. He hadn't forgotten nearly making love to her. He hadn't forgotten admitting he wanted her. He'd never intended to forget or ignore or erase, just . . . deny.

He flashed her just one look, and then his gaze focused on the road. Once he left the parking lot there was no light except that of the twin car beams making yellow patches on black asphalt. "A little adventure put some color in your cheeks. In fact, I think you were in exactly that kind of mood tonight, weren't you? The mood to court a little danger, juggle a little dynamite."

"Clay—"

"You and I go back a long way—and there's absolutely nothing wrong with what happened between us tonight. No one's going to know; no one's going to make too much of it. Friends . . ."

She stopped listening after "friends." She'd heard it before. Gently, quietly, carefully he was yet again trying to tell her that his feelings for her were always going to be those between honorary kid sister and guardian. She turned her head, studying the stubborn angle of his jaw, the shuttered darkness in his eyes. No, Clay. Not this time. I was there, in that water and darkness. When you wanted so much you were shaking with it.

She closed her eyes, resting her head back against the seat. She thought about jumping off cliffs. She considered that no sane woman would make the rational decision of jumping off a cliff. She thought about mistakes she'd made because of choosing rational decisions instead of trusting those instincts.

When he pulled in her drive, she smiled at him. "At least the lights are off in the house. I'm not sure I'm up to explaining to Andy what happened. I'll return the blanket, Clay."

"I'll take care of getting your purse and clothes from the Y in the morn—"

"I love you." She said it short and simple, from the heart, then pecked his cheek and climbed out of the car. Midnight was no time to dawdle in bare feet and a scant blanket. Andy, thank heavens, hadn't locked the back door. Shivering like mad, she let herself in and then leaned against the door with eyes squeezed shut.

She'd seen his expression.

Three simple words, and the man had exhibited instant flu symptoms.


Eight days later, Liz walked out of the chamber of commerce office feeling as if someone had kicked her in the teeth. The November wind slashed at her coat, biting her ears and cheeks. Her shoulders hunched to keep from shivering, she strode down Main Street, passing the hardware, Keeter's dress shop, the bank and Owl Book Store, Nealy's...

She backtracked two steps and pushed through the pharmacy door. Perching on the red vinyl seat at the drugstore counter, she stashed her purse at her feet and waited. Mr. Nealy had other customers.

Nothing had changed since she'd worked here after school as a kid. The soda fountain decor was still red and white. Penny candies were still sold from under a glass counter. Comic books were displayed on a rack in front. Spit-shiny windows viewed Ravensport's river, where this afternoon, the wind had chopped waves into a restless froth.

The view suited her mood just fine, and too clearly reminded her of the potential job she'd just lost. Coming home wasn't easy. She'd returned committed to honestly facing what she wanted and needed in her life, and after weeks of soul-searching, she'd done that. Her ducks were all in line; they just didn't seem to be facing in her direction. She'd discovered a job that mattered terribly to her, only to get turned down after an hour's interview. And she'd faced up to loving Clay, only he was still determined to see her in a prom dress.

*What is it about you, Elizabeth? Your breath?*

The scrawny-haired man with the sagging chin ambled toward her. "Never mind telling me what you want, Elizabeth Brady," the old man rasped. "A double scoop vanilla soda and don't spare the fizz. So what're you waiting for?"

"Pardon?"

"Get yourself up and around the counter. You know your way around back there as well as I do, or you used to. You think I'm going to wait on you when I got serious customers to take care of?"

With a chuckle, Liz grabbed her purse and followed him behind the counter. He pointed at the extra white apron hanging from a hook. She obediently snatched it and slid the long white loop over her head. "Now don't use all the soda," he scolded her.

"Yes, sir."

"Don't be stingy on the ice cream, either."

"Yes, sir."

"And what's that grin all about?"

"I was just remembering how terrified I used to be of you, Mr. Nealy."

"Not near scared enough," Mr. Nealy said feelingly, and gave her a wide berth while he fixed three triple scoop cones for the matched set of towheaded urchins in the corner.

Like riding a bike, Liz hadn't forgotten where the tall stainless pitchers were or how to slam the mixer with the heel of her hand to make it work. The smells of bubbles and vanilla unaccountably lifted her broody mood. Ignoring Mr. Nealy's disapproving glare, she perched on the counter with a spoon—the soda was too thick to draw up with a straw. By that time, he'd finished making sundaes for two teenagers and was wiping the counters.

"Hear much from your parents these days?"

Her tongue was almost too frozen with ice cream to speak. "They're both fine. Both married again."

"So I heard. I still remember how hard you took it as a kid when they split up. Andy serious yet about that red-haired art teacher, or is he just going to keep on dating her for another five years?"

"She doesn't seem to want to settle down."

"She'd settle down just fine if he ever worked up the courage to ask her to. The whole town knows more about how the two of them feel about each other than they do. Young people!" Mr. Nealy shook his head in total disgust. "And I didn't figure it would take you this long to come back home, Elizabeth Brady."

"No?" Her gaze wandered to the windows, and the gray river and fast-moving clouds. There was nothing pretty about Ravensport's river in November. And the fierce wave of love and loyalty for her home almost took her breath away.

While she'd been busy making a disastrous mess of her life in Milwaukee, her town had suffered economic troubles. Enough businesses had moved out to make the chamber of commerce advertise a public relations position—which Liz had been interviewed for that morning. Ravensport had minimal potential as a major port, but it drew boats from Lake Michigan, summer trade. The highway that led from Sheboygan to Milwaukee—where Clay's business thrived—could easily handle more service businesses. Someone had to draw them in. Someone who understood that the townspeople hated neon lights and tinsel and didn't want any new industries that would threaten the feel and nature of a small town.

Someone who wasn't going to be Liz. She'd known that morning that she didn't have the PR degree or experience with people they really wanted. She simply knew she could do it, that she wanted it. Some might not consider the job so exciting, but one man's cup of tea was another's champagne. To shift from a career as a librarian to a sky diver had never been her goal. She wanted challenges and work with people, commitment she could sink her teeth into, work where she felt she could make a difference....

Spilled milk, Elizabeth, she reminded herself. She seemed to have demolished the ice cream in her soda. Sliding down from the counter, she found the glass jar that held the straws, and popped in two of the kind that crinkled near the top.

"Heard you been spending some time with Clay again?" Mr. Nealy never stopped wiping his counters.

"Yes." Liz's smile was wry. To deny her contact with Clay would have been ridiculous. When a body wanted information in Ravensport, they could check the library, the newspaper or Mr. Nealy's pharmacy. Maybe, half-consciously, she'd even stopped here for more than a soda, but she didn't necessarily expect the earful she got.

The town was still slugging gossip where Clay was concerned. Word had it he'd been involved with a married woman two years back, that he'd financed improvements on his place with shady money, and, the worst, that some kid's father had tried to tear up his restaurant. Something about Clay encouraging his kid to try drugs.

Mr. Nealy leveled her a long look, as if expecting her to comment. Liz had known him too long.

"I'm not saying I know what's true and not true. All I do is pass on what I hear, but I also heard he's got a room in that motel he set up for kids in trouble. Drugs, runaways, whatever...they got a place to go. It also could be—I'm not saying it is, but it could be— that Lancer at the bank's got a problem with sour grapes because Clay made good on money Lancer didn't have the sense to loan him at the time. And as far as that married woman nonsense—that scandal came out of Hester McKee. I guess I'd believe anything Hester McKee said when the moon turns green. Now the way I see it ..."

Mr. Nealy gave her ample opportunity to interrupt again, but Liz didn't feel inclined.

"The way I see it," Mr. Nealy repeated, "Clay Stewart never answered to anybody from the time he was four years old, and he still don't. He's been a renegade a hoot of a long time. Hell will freeze over before he defends himself, and there ain't nobody ever going to tell that man what to do or how to do it."

"I know," Liz murmured.

"He's got one Achilles' heel—that boy of his. Anybody give that kid a hard time, I wouldn't want to be around to pick up the pieces when Clay was through with them."

Her eyes turned soft. "I know that, too."

"Myself, I've seen him pick up a beer now and then. One beer, never two. His mother died a few years back, did you know?"

"I heard."

"When the rich get a drinking problem, they call them alcoholics. The poor just get called drunks. Clay's mother could have been a millionaire and she'd never have been more than a drunk. She made darn sure that kid believed nobody ever wanted him." Mr. Nealy never took a breath. "You gonna catch that boy this time, Elizabeth, or you just gonna chase him like you did the last time and then desert the ship?"

Her lips parted in surprise. "What a thing to say! I never 'deserted' Clay, Mr. Nealy."

"No?"

"Of course not. I left home…because it wasn't *like* home once my parents separated. Andy didn't need me around, and I had college to go to, a living to make."

"So that's it, was it? I would have sworn you left home because Clay talked you into leaving." Shrewd eyes settled on her. "I guess I always believed you never wanted to go. 'Course if you never wanted to go, can't imagine why you did. He thought the sun rose and set with you. You must have known that."

Mr. Nealy's prying had gone too far. If she'd cared for him any less, she'd have said so. "You've misunderstood. Or have you forgotten that ten years ago I was just a girl? A girl who made a habit of tagging after him, just like you said," she said softly, honestly. "He didn't care for me, Mr. Nealy, not in the way you seem to be implying."

"No?"

Liz took her tall glass to the sink and started rinsing it. "Obviously not," she said blithely.

"By 'obviously,' you must have added two and two and come up with his son. And you're absolutely right about that, Elizabeth."

"Right about what?" she asked impatiently. She loved Mr. Nealy, she'd loved the soda. She knew darn well that walking in here was the same as inviting a personal grilling and she'd wanted to hear about Clay. Now, though, she had the fast urge to be alone.

"You were right about how long it takes to make a baby," he said smoothly. "Right about how fast he got involved with other women after you left. There were lots of women, each more bad news than the last, not one he gave a hoot in hell about. A body might be inclined to think the man had a big problem with hurt, but I guess a woman wouldn't see it that way." He frowned. "Pick up your purse to pay for that soda and you'll get your hand slapped, Elizabeth Brady."

She gave Mr. Nealy a resounding smack on his cheek that turned his ears red, and left. She'd listened long enough. Too long. In the past hour, the sky had turned an ominous charcoal. She barely noticed, head down as she hurried the three blocks toward her car.

Mr. Nealy meant well. He simply had everything wrong. She hadn't left Ravensport because of Clay. Thoughts of his other women had never bothered her. And as far as Clay thinking the sun rose and set with her, well, Mr. Nealy should have been around for the past eight days.

She'd had the idea that telling Clay she loved him might provoke a reaction from him. It certainly had. For the entire past week, he'd shown up twice a day instead of once, usually with his son. A little basketball, a little football, bike rides, hikes. Liz had stopped worrying that Spence might build up expectations from spending so much time with her. Three-person football games could destroy any child's illusions that his father was romantically involved.

She had to give him credit, Clay never avoided trouble. Straight up, he'd treated her with wonderful patience and kindness, the same way he'd treat someone who saw UFO's. One doesn't try to reason with the demented. One physically exhausts them to keep their mind off their delusions.

Liz was exhausted. Not hurt.

Mr. Nealy was wrong about everything.

And you're still a liar, she thought wearily.

Her heart kept whispering that he needed someone, that no one had ever been around for Clay when the chips were down, that for all the women in his life, no one had ever forced that man to take love, affection, warmth.

The thought of other women in his life darn near killed her. For that matter, something was ridiculously wrong with the entire female population in Ravensport if no one had seen yet what that man *did* need. A strong, giving woman. A woman who didn't back down from honesty and real emotion. A woman who didn't let pride stand in the way of what she knew, what she felt, what she wanted for herself. And for him.

What ever happened to faith in yourself, Elizabeth Brady? she thought as her step unaccountably faltered in front of the sign that read Kaiser's. She felt the oddest impulse to push open the door. Are you going to believe him, Liz? Or are you going to believe in what you know happens every time you touch each other?

Brooding was tiresome. What she needed, she decided, was a mood lift. The same mood lift women had been choosing since the beginning of time. Change. Impulse. Risk. Wasn't that what she'd come home for?

Pushing aside a dozen rational misgivings, Liz dredged up her courage and opened the door.

# Seven

"Like it?" Janet Kaiser asked from behind her. "I think the style's perfect for you. Lots of body, easy to take care of." The hairdresser untied the plastic apron from around Liz's neck. Clumps of pale gold hair drifted to the floor. Lots of clumps.

Blindly ignoring the mirror, Liz stepped down from the chair. The new style was French, breezy and short. Wisps of bangs spiked her forehead. A toss of her head and the whole thing moved. The look was sassy and sexy, the kind a bold, confident woman would choose. Or the look a woman might choose if she was hoping to talk herself into bold confidence.

"You like it, don't you?" Janet sounded anxious.

"Hmm," Liz murmured enthusiastically. Holy petunias, she looked as if she'd just climbed out of a man's bed. How could she possibly go out in public? Was there a miracle glue for hair?

She paid the woman, added a generous tip—panic pay—and forced her cropped head out the door. The late afternoon was ominously dark for only five o'clock. When she glanced up, she felt the season's first wet, white splash of snow on her cheeks.

By the time she arrived home, the few drifting flakes had turned into a white deluge. Turning up her coat collar, she raced past Andy's car for the door.

Thankfully the back hall was lit and warm. She ducked her head into the kitchen. Her brother was wearing a jacket and pouring milk in a small glass, both of which struck her as strange. "Are you just going out?" she asked him.

"Thank heavens you're here! I just came in five minutes ago, and..." Andy glanced up. "Good Lord, what did you do to your hair?"

Trust a brother to send a woman's ego to the pits. She motioned to his glass. "What is this, a new fad? I haven't seen you drink milk since you were ten years old."

"It's not for me. You had a package waiting for you on the doorstep when I drove in."

"A package?"

"We have a crisis," Andy mouthed to her.

She could see that the minute she walked in the den. The crisis was about four feet tall, with a manic cowlick, hunched shoulders and a spray of freckles that looked disastrously dark against a too white face. Spence was draped on the ottoman, his miserable brown eyes staring at her. "Spence! Sweetheart, what are you doing here? How did you—?"

"I can't go home.

"Milk." Liz reached back for the glass in Andy's hand like a surgeon for a scalpel. "Come on now. What could possibly be that bad?"

"Everything." Spence's voice spelled gloom. He took three chugs of milk with the desperation of a milkaholic. The resulting white mustache didn't age him any. "I'm going to have to come live with you. It's the only way."

"Trouble in school?" Liz added delicately. She dropped her coat to the couch and sat down.

Spence heaved out the words. "I got a letter from the principal I'm supposed to give to my dad. Only I can't. *Ever*."

"Pretty bad, hmm?"

Tears started to splash and the story came out fast. He'd skipped math class by sitting on a toilet in the boy's bathroom with his feet up so no one could find him if they looked at the floor under the stall. That struck Liz as brilliantly resourceful for a half-pint third-grader, but then Spence had Clay's genes—and Clay's love of trouble. That wasn't the full extent of his problem in school.

He intended to skip more classes. In fact, he'd told the principal that he intended to skip math for the rest of his life, which seemed to have irritated his principal. A lot.

Liz mopped Spence's eyes and listened, trying not to smile. He sounded so much like his father. As far as she could figure out—Spence's story was slightly garbled—the real problem was that Spence was ahead of the other kids in math. "So my dad and this principal got together and had this big talk about *challenging*," he said disgustedly. "You know what that word means?"

To Spence, the word meant that he was moved into the sixth grade during math hour. Algebra was neat, but Spence didn't want to be with the sixth-graders. He kept forgetting the sixth grade teacher's name and he was afraid to ask to go to the bathroom. In his class, in the third grade, he got to go around during math helping everybody else. "The older kids call me a 'brain' and I have to sit in this desk where my feet don't even reach. I'm not going back there!"

Liz held the tissue in front of his nose so he could blow. "Sweetheart, why didn't you just tell your dad you were unhappy ages ago?" She looked up to find Andy still in the doorway, arms folded across his chest and a compassionate twinkle in his eyes. Over Spence's shoulder, she whispered, "Would you call Clay again and tell him we'll be a little longer?"

"I couldn't tell Dad. I still can't tell Dad. I'll never be able to tell my dad. He was the one who wanted this challenging stuff. . . ."

Liz saw the mix of guilt and surprise on Andy's face, and felt her heart stop. Until then, it had never occurred to her that Andy *hadn't* immediately called Clay when he found Spence at their house. "I'll call him now," Andy said swiftly. "The thing was, I'd just gotten home minutes before you did, and when I saw Spence, he was sitting on the porch in the snow. All I really thought about was getting him warm and dry. Then you walked in—"

"I understand," Liz said, but all she could think about was the time—twenty minutes after five—and that Clay must have been expecting his son home from school two hours earlier.

Spence had stopped talking. "You can't call my dad!"

"Honey, I have to. Try and imagine how worried he is, not knowing where you are."

"I know how mad he's going to be," Spence said glumly. "Couldn't I just stay here? Sleep on the couch?"

Liz kept her left arm around his shoulder while she dialed with her right hand. Susie, the desk clerk, answered the phone, but her voice was replaced by Clay's in the space of a second. Liz didn't waste time on casual greetings. "He's absolutely fine, Clay, and I'm bringing him home," she said shortly.

When she hung up the phone, she couldn't remember a thing he'd said. The agony of tension in his voice had seared through her. Lions never misplaced their cubs. Especially not that lion.

And the lion's son was staring at her with woebegone eyes.

"Listen, you." Liz bent down to kiss his forehead, then grabbed their coats. "You're absolutely right, he's a little upset. I'm not going to fib. All dads get upset when they don't know where their kids are. You know darn well your dad loves you to bits, so what's the big deal?''

"You're coming home with me?"

"Zip up your jacket; it's freezing out there. And of course I'm coming home with you...."

"The last time I was late from school, Dad called the police and state troopers."

Liz could well believe that. Not until she was behind the wheel did she realize how hard her heart was pounding. The windshield wipers creaked and the snow kept falling, fast and wet. She kept up a steady reassuring monologue for Spence. The little one was so sure she was coming for him.

She wasn't. Whether or not Spence believed it, he didn't need ballast in his court. Clay had a temper and was more than capable of a teapot blow—a lot of heat and sound that fizzled out very quickly—but no one could be safer or more loved than Spence when he was with his dad.

She wasn't coming for Spence, but for Clay. Just for once, she had the feeling he might need someone.

Heaven knew who was running the motel. The instant Liz and Spence stepped into the lobby, George appeared from the bar, Susie left the front desk, the chef had obviously been looking for an excuse to desert the kitchens, and Cameron—well, Cameron had been pacing the lobby with Clay, so he had an excuse for being there. The group clustered around Spence so fast you'd have thought they were protecting him from

Jack's giant. That urchin was eating up the attention, telling his afternoon's adventures.

Clay wanted his hands on his son, yet he stayed back for those few seconds, too aware that his emotions were jammed on overload. His pulse was still ticking like a bomb, his heart still slamming against his chest. Yeah, he'd known Spence was safe from the moment Liz called, but he'd been swamped with visions of kidnappers and child abusers from the minute Spence hadn't shown up on the school bus.

For a man who never acknowledged fear, Clay could still feel the terror ripping him apart. And in those long minutes before he'd heard from Liz, his failures had gnawed at him. Other people—the kind with regular jobs and backyards with swing sets and holiday traditions where relatives came all the way from Timbuktu—those were the kind who were supposed to raise kids. Inadequacies ate at him, for what he hadn't given Spence. For what he couldn't.

The Red Sea of bodies parted to let a small blond woman through, closing immediately again on his son. Liz hesitated a moment, and then surged toward him. If ever a man looked alone in a crowd, it was Clay. With his hands hooked on his belt, his shoulders thrown back, and his jaw rigid, he radiated cold hard anger. Only Liz saw his eyes, clear and deep, wild and lonely.

Brazen as you please, she raised up on tiptoe to kiss him. "He's fine, Clay. Try to believe it."

"I can see he's fine." He could also feel something ease inside him that he didn't want eased, simply from the touch of her. Something about Elizabeth Brady was clearly dangerous to Stewart men. Spence had taken one look and adopted her. Clay took one look and felt sanity slipping.

Beneath her flopping coat, her dress was red—Liz never wore red. And her hair—he could have killed her. You don't cut silver; you invest in it. Now there were undisciplined strands wisping on her forehead. The sassy fluff was styled to catch the wind, invite a man's hands to touch and play. Her throat looked naked.

She made him feel helpless with the red dress and the haircut, her talk of fast changes and her wild rush to experience new things. He knew she hadn't meant that rash declaration of love.

There were only two people in his life who had ever mattered to him. He never seemed to do the right thing by either one of them. With Liz, all he wanted to do was protect her from the wrong kind of man until she was over the new-divorced syndrome. Instead, his instinct to protect increasingly dissolved into need, desire and a fierce lonely yearning that twisted guilt inside him.

He hadn't meant to say anything about Spence at this moment, but the words snapped out because of the despair he felt. "I could have sworn he knew he could always come to me, no matter what kind of trouble he was in. What the hell did he think I was going to do?"

"He doesn't think you're going to do anything, Clay. Except yell at him, and that's not what he's afraid of."

"Well, what is he afraid of then?"

Liz touched his cheek. As with everything else, when Clay hurt, he hurt hard, unreasonably and far too deeply. He didn't seem to realize how tightly he was gripping her hand. "He never said it in so many words, but I'm fairly sure he's terrified of disappointing you."

"That's the stupidest thing I ever heard!"

"You may have to mention that to him."

"I'll do more than *mention* it to him."

Clay certainly strode toward the crowd with rage in his expression, but that was worth as much as island property in Arizona. The crowd moved aside, and then he had his hands on his son. Shoulders, spine, knees, freckles, sturdy bones and cowlicks . . . he had to reassure himself that his son was all there before his eyes closed and he spun Spence up and high.

Liz could feel Clay inhaling the smell, feel, taste, sound, sight of his son.

"*You*," Clay leveled at Spence, "are in a lot of trouble!"

The boy pushed back from his father's stranglehold, far enough back to study Clay's face. Worried brown eyes registered amazement. "You're not mad."

"You gotta be kidding. I am roaring mad at you."

"Come on, Dad, I can see you're not. Hurry up and put me down. People are gonna think I'm a kid!"

"Tough luck." Clay shifted his son to one arm and grabbed Liz's hand—Liz seemed to have some idiotic idea about melting into the nearest potted palm. Abruptly he was aware that a lobby full of people seemed to be smiling at him. Cameron's grin was plain silly. A perfectly strange woman was sitting on a suitcase with her husband, smiling to beat the band. The staff, people waiting to check in—what'd they think this was, a set for *Father Knows Best*? Three sets of phones were ringing and the restaurant was filling up with the dinner crowd. "No one has anything to do?" Clay barked.

Bodies scattered. He had the only two that mattered chained to him as he stalked down the corridor to his apartments. His son gained five pounds every yard. He was also sporting a relieved grin and an increasingly cocky sparkle in his eyes—which unfortunately wouldn't last long. When Spence hadn't shown up on the bus, Clay had called the school.

"All right. Where's the note?" he demanded once they were safely locked in his place.

"What note?" Spence took another glance at his dad's face and murmured, "Oh, that note. The one Liz is going to explain to you."

"Liz is going to be busy taking off her shoes and crashing on that couch. She's had a tough afternoon. You'll have to do the explaining yourself. But first, I want to know exactly how you got to Liz's place."

"I took the school bus. I just got off at her corner instead of coming all the way home." That his father had been concerned about transportation had obviously never crossed Spence's mind.

"And the driver just let you do that?"

Spence looked bewildered. "Why should he care?"

Liz glanced at Clay and thought wryly that the bus driver would care terribly, as of tomorrow, about where and when he let off the next school kid. Spence never saw the play of emotion in his father's eyes, he was too busy worrying the note that Clay now had in his hand.

While Clay read it, she slipped off her shoes and padded in stocking feet behind the couch where he was sitting. The cords in his neck were taut enough to line a ruler. She went to work with the tips of her fingers. He reached back with a hand as if he would brush aside a fly, and all she could think of was that no one was supposed to touch Clay when he was hurting. No one was supposed to come close. Everybody was supposed to scatter like wheat in the wind for one of his dangerous scowls.

Clay lived by an idiotic set of rules. Almost as idiotic as the ones she used to live by. Spence had draped himself over the top of the opposite couch as if he hoped his dad might mistake him for an afghan.

Clay finished the note and crooked his finger at his son.

"I think I should go do my homework now."

Clay's forefinger kept motioning him closer, and Spence started spouting explanations a mile a minute. By the time the long school tale was finished, Spence was talking from Clay's lap, knees scrunched up and elbows jutting out.

"You goofed," Clay said gently.

"Hell, I know that."

"Not because of what you said to the principal, although that's obviously going to take a two-man apology in the morning. And not because of skipping out of class. You goofed, Spence, because when you're in trouble you bring it home and you own up. Why the he—sam hill didn't you tell me you were miserable in that math class?"

"Because."

"Because why?"

"Because you *wanted* me in that math class," Spence said miserably.

"You're out of your tree. I only set that up because I thought you liked it. Your teacher said you were bored, that you were way ahead of the other kids, that you'd like it more if you were challenged. If you didn't like it, all you had to do was tell me."

"But you like it that I'm smart," Spence said.

"Boy, do you have that one wrong. I like it when you're happy."

"I'd be a helluva lot happier if I didn't have to go into that sixth grade every day."

"The next time you see sixth grade, you'll be in it. So if that's all settled, we've only got two more things we have to talk about." His son was squirming on his lap like ants over jam. "First, I thought we both agreed to give up swearing."

"I'm trying!"

"So am I and it's by jiminy by crackers a devil a lot harder when you've been doing it for twenty years. Second . . ." Clay's voice lowered to a painful whisper. "Dammit, Spence, were you really afraid to come to me?"

Spence worried out the words. "It wasn't that I was afraid of your yelling. I was afraid you'd feel bad about me."

"That's not possible," Clay informed him.

"Okay. Dad, I have to feed my fish now."

Clay claimed a hug and let him loose. As soon as Spence was out of sight, he let out a long exhausted breath, only then aware that Liz was drawing on her coat. "Where are you going?"

"Home." She felt odd, like walking on tiptoe. Maybe if she breathed just right and got out of there fast, Clay just might discover that he'd accepted comfort from her. The comfort of a kiss, a touch, of someone there when he was troubled. She swung her purse strap to her shoulder. "You handled your son beautifully."

"I didn't. If I was handling him right, he'd have known he could come to me."

"That's nonsense. You ever met a child who wasn't in a fast hurry to avoid a scold?"

"Sometimes I'm afraid he's slightly on the spoiled side."

"Of course he is. You had it tough as a kid, you're always going to overcompensate. Don't you think that's human nature?"

"A lot of people in this town don't think a motel's a fit place to raise a kid."

"A lot of people are bananas. It's a terrific place for him to grow up, Clay. Even in your busiest times, you're only seconds away from him in an emergency, and he's got all these extra caretakers around—Cam and George and Susie. They all adore him. For Spence it must be like having aunts and uncles around all the time."

He saw her buttoning the top button of her coat, and lurched off the couch like lightning. He should have known better than to start talking with her about Spence. Liz inevitably saw the idealistic and the positive sides of life—and of him. That was exactly what drew him to loving her, exactly why he kept his distance. She believed in him like a blind vulnerable kitten. Sometimes he wanted to shout at her to see him as he was, less than a hero and a man who'd often failed, a man who'd made ugly mistakes.

Only he didn't really want her to see him that way. He didn't really want her to see Clay Stewart. It wasn't honorable or honest or moral or right, but part of him wanted the illusion as long as he could hold it. The illusion of her loving him.

She could tie him up in knots with the simple act of pulling on her gloves. He wanted her to leave. His head was desperately clicking off ways to make her stay. "You had a job interview today?"

"Yes."

"Care to mention how it went?"

"No," she said simply. It wasn't the first time they had discussed this.

"You've been remarkably quiet on the wheres and hows and whens of your job hunting."

"Because if I told you I was having trouble, you'd help me. One of these days, I'm hoping you're going to notice that I'm past my prom dress days and fully capable of handling my own problems." She smiled, noting without surprise that his mouth was already parting with denials and objections and questions.

She chose the easy way to forestall that nonsense, and she could count the barriers going up when she reached up and kissed him. The shoulders stiffened. Heat flooded his body. Fingers gripped her shoulders to carefully maintain distance. She understood all the body language. Guardians didn't kiss their wards.

Sometime soon she was going to have to tell him that his mouth gave him away. She tasted loneliness every time. Her fingers drifted his hair, anchoring him where she wanted him. His mouth shifted under hers. Tongue found tongue and he was suddenly drinking of that intimacy.

She gradually pulled back, feeling shock waves of longing to stay. That wouldn't do. Pushing Clay wasn't wise and she felt as if she'd won rainbows as it was.

"Sunshine . . ." His voice was a thread of a growl.

"How could anyone not love you?"

Like a firefly, there was just that spark of incendiary danger—that sweet, that bright, that helplessly fragile—and then she was gone.

* * *

Clay sampled his chef's new recipe for filet of sole medallion, and worried about where Liz was, what she was doing, whom she was with. "Delicious," he admitted. "But I still think it's too fancy for the bread-and-butter crowd."

"They could learn to like it," Ralph insisted.

"Maybe." Maybe she'd gone for another evening swim, and maybe not alone. The thought made him violently ill. Spence trailed behind him, a gulf shrimp in one hand and a stuffed baked potato in the other.

Sometime he was going to have to tell Spence that normal people didn't eat standing up, in a kitchen the size of a warehouse, with a handful of kitchen staff who made a bended-knee production out of coaxing him to try vegetables.

"The smoked ham's perfect tonight, Ralph."

Ralph beamed. Spence swallowed a mouthful, and piped out, "Are you going to marry Liz?"

"What?"

"I asked you if you were going to marry Liz."

The spoonful of soup Clay had been sampling went back in the pot. Busboys were remarkably and suddenly still. Ralph didn't seem to have a thing to do. "What on earth kind of question is that?" Clay whispered sotto voce.

Spence shrugged, his mouth full of sour cream and melted butter. "I know you always said we weren't going to marry anyone. But we don't usually take girls to play football with us, either. Or take 'em around, like on Halloween."

Ralph had a coughing fit. Clay glared at him. His son did pick his times. "You do that kind of thing with *friends*. Friends are people who may come and go in your life, but you still care about them. We already talked about that."

"So..." Spence appeared to consider. "Liz is a friend?"

"Exactly."

"And you're not going to marry her?"

"No."

"Then I am." Spence glanced at a pot, recognized broccoli and grimaced.

"I think you're a little young for marriage," Clay said gravely. "Also, last I knew you weren't too fond of the whole female species."

"You mean girls? I hate girls. But Liz isn't like *women,* dad. Liz is just Liz." Spence licked the bottom of the spoon, and then brightened for the tray of pastries. "She likes kids, you know."

"I know, sport."

"So if she marries someone besides you and me, she could have kids. Kids that aren't me. I don't think that's such a good idea."

Clay scowled at the grin on this chef's face. "What do you mean 'she could have kids'?"

"Dad, gimme a break. I've watched Phil Donahue. I know all about that stuff."

"Wait a minute." Spence's face was plastered with chocolate. Clay reached for a napkin. "When did you watch Phil Donahue?"

"When I was home from school and had a stomachache. Don't you remember? Anyway—" Spence licked his fingers around his father's napkin-wiping "—the way I see it, one of us has to marry her. And if it's not going to be you, it has to be me. Hey—"

Clay stopped the five rabid fingers from reaching for an éclair. "We're going back to the room."

"Why?"

Because his son was catching it: that obsession that came with the Stewart genes to protect Liz, the panic at the idea of her involvement with other men, having children by other men, attracting other men.

Clay had to get his mind off her.

His son wasn't helping.

# Eight

---

Clay had barely gotten his jacket off before a brunette in a red spangled top had hooked her arms around his neck and delivered an openmouthed smack on his lips. Another full-bodied creature with wild hair handed him a beer. Somewhere a record was blaring an old one about "fever," and the smoke hit him in waves before he ever found his way to the living room. He'd forgotten that parties at Speed Matthews's house tended to get out of hand.

Getting a little out of hand suited Clay's mood just fine. He hadn't spent anytime with the old crowd—Tom, Frank, Speed—in years. If all three were married now and toting mortgages, it didn't show when they were putting on a gig. Their kids were stashed somewhere. Liquor was flowing freely. If he felt a flash of weariness at the decibel level, he ignored it. "What's happened to you? You too high and mighty for the rest of us?" Matthews had asked him, when he'd been about to refuse yet another invitation. He wasn't.

A brunette wearing a silver blouse sidled next to him and slid her arm around his waist. "Haven't seen you in a blue moon, Clay." He knew her from somewhere. His impulse was to stiffen from the contact and cloying perfume, but he didn't. He wasn't too high and mighty for that, either. The day he grew too fuddy-duddy to enjoy appreciation in a woman's eyes, the sway of sultry lips and come-on lips—well, he wasn't, that was all.

He also knew the brunette's game. One night with someone was better than one more night of silence. No strings, no expectations, no judgments made. Clay knew the rules because he'd been playing them all his life. The brunette was the kind who understood the man he was and wasn't.

Mentally, emotionally and physically Clay was well aware he'd been celibate ever since a pint-size blonde had come home. Dangerous business, celibacy. It occurred to Clay that one night with another woman— any woman—might be the only cure for this obsession he had with wanting Elizabeth Brady.

He talked a few more minutes with the brunette, and then murmured, "I'll be back. I'm going to get another beer."

He took a slow route back to the kitchen, annoyingly aware that his beer was full and that he felt relief once the woman was out of sight. A clutch of men were in the kitchen. Tom had a paunch these days. Speed was already two sheets to the wind and making a pitcher of rum swizzles. Both men clapped him on the back and started talking old times until the laughter grew raucous. They shared memories of cruising Ravensport Main Street looking for action, memories of girls, of climbing the old fire tower and the police catching them and of one hell of a chase.

Clay remembered to contribute in the right places, laugh at the right times. Claustrophobia started to nag at him, a welling feeling of isolation. Shut up, Stewart, a voice inside him nagged. You think you can't have fun just because a brown-eyed princess isn't standing near you?

Tom's wife popped in, a frizzy redhead with an overstacked upstairs and nothing much in her brain. She threw herself at Clay with a resounding hug. "Clay, good to see you!" He grinned down at her upturned face, too aware of her bouncing breasts against his chest. Carrie had come on to him before. Maybe he felt nothing in common with the old gang anymore, but she was still Tom's wife. Her fingers slid down to his hips. He felt abruptly sickened.

"Well..." He eased to a straighter posture. "Can't stand here jawing forever. Got a lady waiting for me in the other room."

"Just one? You're slipping in your old age, Stewart," Speed teased him.

He knew that. He stood in the hall wondering where he could find less noise, less smoke, less confusion, and thought, you're having a good time, Stewart. And you're going to realize that just as soon as you get Liz off your mind.

The noise level doubled when additional partyers entered the front door. He leaned in the doorway, the beer tipped to his lips when he noticed the three women shedding their coats. The three had been in the same class at school together, he remembered, which had nothing to do with the sudden tight feeling in his throat. He recognized the flash of brown eyes, the silky swish of short silver-blond hair.

Liz didn't belong in this crowd. Her choice of caramel sweater and white crepe pants was demure, the pearls in her ears a murmur of softness next to a room filled with razzle-dazzle rhinestones. Her cheeks had windswept color instead of paint and her lips were touched with muted coral. It took Clay all of a second and a half to want her with a force that infuriated him. More than that, he could see the sparkle in her eyes had a hint of reckless, a hint of haunted.

She was up to more trouble, he thought glumly. Not oysters this time, no crazy haircuts or impulsively moving home. Not mysterious career changes or whimsical declarations of love designed to drive a man mad—and Liz was awfully good at driving a man mad. She could make a man feel as if the only thing between him and a Siberia of cold emptiness was a pair of soft brown eyes.

A redhead spotted him. Clay winked to be polite and then ducked. He emerged from the crowd—by accident—standing just behind Liz. In that second's breath she turned, her lips on the rim of a glass of one of Speed's dangerous rum sizzlers, and glanced up.

"Watch those, sunshine. They're lethal."

"Clay!" Liz could barely make herself heard over the noise. "Lord, it's wild in here."

She looked happy about that, which earned her a glare from a pair of narrowed eyes. Liz didn't see that. One of the old schoolmates she'd come with grabbed her arm and dragged her closer to the music. Someone had rolled up a rug.

Clay saw her kick off her shoes. Speed whirled her around the makeshift dance floor, then Frank, then a lanky fellow he didn't know. He heard her laughter, saw her flushed face.

Liz didn't know who put the second rum sizzler in her hands, but then she hadn't noticed who gave her the first. Twice, she tried to find Clay again. But the first time he seemed barricaded in a corner with a witchy brunette, the second time his arm was slung around a well-endowed redhead.

They finally met on an in-and-out at the bathroom, Liz coming out, Clay going in. "Isn't it a wonderful party?" she enthused.

"Wonderful," he agreed. "You seem to be having a good time."

"Almost as much as you." He smiled easily, like old friends. She smiled back the same way.

By midnight, she'd escaped to the kitchen and seemed to be talking to a guy in glasses with the build of a runner and the nose of a fox. Heaven knew what he was talking about. Her head hurt from the constant noise and something was shattering inside of her, piece by piece.

There wasn't a woman at the party who hadn't gotten her hands on Clay but her. Party behavior wasn't like life, of course. Heck, if Liz hadn't wanted to kick up her heels a little, she'd have stayed home and knitted socks.

"...you want to come back to my place?"

"Hmm?" She glanced up, smiled distractedly at Fox Nose and went back to her brooding.

All she could think about were the times she and Clay had almost made love. Almost. And all those bold assertive women at the party with their hands all over him. He certainly hadn't been fighting them very hard.

"I think you're beautiful."

"Fascinating," Liz murmured brightly.

Clay only seemed to blow hot or cold for her. She'd already duly considered whether it was her breath, her looks, her toothpaste. She'd spent a lot of time well aware Clay still had lingering feelings about her as an honorary kid sister. Only what happened when they touched was as volatile and primeval and basic and fantastic as man and woman.

For her, at least.

The idea that he gave in to all that volatile and primeval and basic with other women was a pleasant thought. Like catching the flu was a pleasant thought.

Clay was passing the kitchen doorway when he saw John Greeley's arm reach out to drape Liz's neck. The distance across the kitchen floor was four feet. He spanned it in three quarters of a second. "Had enough of the party?"

"Pardon?"

"Nancy and Janet left, Liz. I told them I'd give you a ride home. You ready to go?"

It was cold outside. A fresh snow had brightened the night. The soft fluff curled in windowsills like whipped cream, made smooth white lakes of the lawns.

Liz huddled in her coat, shivering while Clay turned the ignition key. The defroster blasted cold air that echoed the general temperament in the car. Not that she minded leaving the party, but Clay had all but railroaded her out the door. His face was immobile and he took the first turn at Indy 500 speed.

"Known him long?" he asked casually.

"Known who long?"

"John Greeley."

She strove for patience. "Clay, who is John Greeley?"

He shot her a look. "Nothing wrong with kicking up your heels, sunshine. I wasn't criticizing. But dammit, not with him."

It looked as if she would have to strive for a little more patience. "What on earth are you talking about?"

They reached her driveway in record time. If the police weren't asleep by this time of night in Ravensport, Liz had no doubt Clay would have had a speeding ticket. She assumed he was miffed because he'd had to leave the party to give her a ride. Since she hadn't asked for a ride—and for a few other reasons—she felt miffed. Except that irritation wasn't quite what she saw in his eyes when he turned to her, the exhausted white lines around his mouth illuminated by street lamps, his gentleness when he turned off the engine and touched her cheek with the knuckles of his hand.

"You're the best woman I know, Elizabeth Brady," Clay said quietly. "And what I'm talking about is finding a man who's good enough for you. You came home needing someone to give to, because that's the kind of woman you are. It's a beautiful quality in you, a special quality, and it's not that I think you don't know your own mind, Liz. Only that anyone can lose perspective when they're going through a rough time. When you make it through this, you'll find him. The right man. A man who's good enough for a lady, a man who can give you what you really need and want."

Liz took a long look at Clay, tried to say something and instead pushed the door handle and climbed out of the car.

Andy's light was off upstairs, and enough dishes were piled in the sink that Liz guessed he'd had his art teacher over for the evening. Still wearing her coat, she

started filling the sink with water and suds. She
popped in two glasses, two plates, two sets of silver-
ware.

Seconds later, she found herself staring out the front
picture window in the living room, hands dripping,
dishes not touched. She'd walked in from Clay's car
confused, vaguely aware that he must have been talking about the man with the fox nose at the party.

Small mental wheels kept clicking in her head, and
they had nothing to do with a stranger she'd spent five
minutes with in a kitchen. All this time. All this time
she'd thought Clay had pulled back from an adult relationship between them because he didn't return her
feelings, because he still saw her as an honorary kid
sister.

Not because he'd put her on some nonsense pedestal called "Lady."

Never because he thought he wasn't good enough
for her.


At two in the morning Clay was still sipping decaf,
thumbing through a catalog on computers that Spence
had left tactfully in a strategic place—propped on his
chair. Disk drives, ROM and RAM and bytes.... If
Spence wanted the darn thing he could have it, as long
as he could decipher the Greek of computer lingo.

Clay couldn't. He tossed down the catalog and
lurched out of the chair, pushing the hair back from
his forehead. Had he gotten through to her? He turned
off the light, then the overhead in the kitchenette, then
checked on Spence.

His son was dead to the world. He was also smothering under too many blankets. Clay fussed with them, closed the door to his son's room and informed himself that he was tired.

He wasn't in the least tired. He tried a shower, then climbed into bed and punched on the tube. Where was a good blood-and-guts flick when a man needed one?

What was he supposed to do, let a loser like Greeley come on to Liz and do nothing about it? Sure, she was entitled to flirt. Her dancing, chatter, flirting with other men seemed good healthy signs that her crush on Clay Stewart was finally fading. Sooner or later she was bound to see that love was only an illusion for a man like him. She deserved more in her life than that.

He'd been very happy to see her come alive at that party.

Very happy.

As if someone had slammed him in the gut.

He was just turning off the television when he heard the soft rap on the door, and hurriedly grabbed a robe. Middle-of-the-night interruptions came with the motel business. This night he welcomed one, but could never have expected the nature of interruption he found at the door.

Liz's face was pale, her eyes distressed, and her hair was dancing with snow diamonds, all wind-tangled and awry. "May I come in?"

"Honey, what's wrong?"

Her arms wrapped her coat closed and her fingers were as cold as ice. She walked in slowly, hearing the concern in his voice and seeing the tired shadows under his eyes. She'd driven here breaking all speed limits, very sure of what she wanted to do, what she needed to do. None of that had changed, but she seemed to have left both nerve and courage in the car.

"Liz—"

"I need to talk to you."

"Something happened?"

"Yes." She glanced at Spence's door. "I wouldn't want to wake him up, Clay."

"Come on."

With a hand at her back, he steered her through the far door to his bedroom/office. Like the spider to the fly, she thought with a wild trace of humor. He latched the door and motioned her to his oversize office chair. "You want coffee?"

"No." His desk was cluttered with papers and files, illuminated by the light by his bed. The covers were tossed up on that double mattress. If he hadn't been sleeping, he must have been trying to. Clay eased down on the corner of the mattress, his gaze still on her face. His robe was a wine-colored velour, old, rumpled and loosely open to the waist.

That she could see his near nakedness, or the implications of the mattress, hadn't occurred to him. He was prepared to talk, to listen. He was prepared to help her, the way Clay had always been prepared to help, to take her side, to take on her troubles.

She could have shaken him.

"Sit down. You look so upset."

"I am." She took a long breath. "I want to talk to you about what you said in the car, Clay. But not quite yet. For a few minutes I don't want to talk at all."

"Liz—"

When she pushed off her coat and dropped it, he abruptly stopped talking. Undoubtedly part of the reason she had such a problem with chill was the basic attire she'd worn here.

Once she slipped off her shoes, she wasn't wearing anything but French panties and a camisole, both in black satin. At home, those choices had seemed to make a very clear statement about ladies. Black satin had always separated the good girls from the bad. Black satin seemed an ideal way to get a woman knocked off a pedestal.

Shock initially made Clay's features immobile. His gaze rippled over black satin, over marble cold skin, up to her eyes. Even a flash of desire would have soothed her nerves a little. Instead, she saw a man's smile, and nothing to relieve the sudden tension in that room but the old thickness in his voice. "Put your coat back on, Elizabeth Brady."

She shook her head, halfway between a rock and a hard place. Her feet didn't want to move forward. She wasn't going back. Clay stood up and started pulling the comforter off the bed.

"Well, you're not going to stand there and freeze to death."

So reasonable, his voice. Patient, reasonable and firm, which was what finally unglued her feet and her nerves. When he turned with the bulky comforter in his hands, she pulled the camisole over her head.

"Dammit, Liz." He dropped the comforter when her fingers started to peel off the French panties. She gave up. Her fingers were shaking too hard. What had she expected him to do, melt into a pile of mindless desire because he had a naked woman on his hands? Obviously Clay had seen his share of naked women. Flesh was flesh, and hers was skinnier than most.

It would have helped if she had a very sexual feeling running around her own bloodstream, but the only thing zooming up and down her veins was a fine building rage. Not good enough for her? You'll find him, Liz. A good man.

What did he think he was, horse meat?

Dammit, she didn't know how she'd gotten on that crazy pedestal to begin with. Fallible. She'd excelled in making mistakes for years. Heck, most of them had been around Clay. True, the ones that really mattered recently had been with David. The ones that mattered related to a woman who could have lied for a profession, who'd never had the courage to admit what she wanted and needed, who'd always been too scared to put herself on the line.

She was on the line now, and had never felt more scared in her life. So, she was slowly coming to understand, was Clay. She decided to scare him a great deal more before this night was over, and she made massive inroads when she moved close enough to touch his cheek.

He had a muscle in that cheek that suddenly tightened. "No, honey," he said quietly. "I mean it,
Liz—"

She knew he did. When she pressed up on tiptoe and
slid both arms around his neck, the temperature in his
whole body changed. Softly, so softly, she touched her
lips to his, as an experienced man might coax a virgin. The image of Clay as a virgin pleased her, gave her
courage. He was, in a sense. She doubted any woman
had invaded certain private territories of Clay. Sex was
something else. She was talking about making very
sure she knew he was...wonderful. A hero. A special
man. A fallible, headstrong, stubborn, overprotective man who deserved much love.

She forgot fears, exercised patience. The tip of her
tongue traced the shape of his mouth. He never
moved. Her tongue traced the rigid line sealing his lips
closed, her fingers sifted up, into his hair. Black satin
brushed his thighs. His heartbeat turned skittery.

"Open your mouth, Clay," she whispered. "I swear
this isn't going to hurt near as much as you're afraid
of."

"Hurt?" He swallowed the lump in his throat.
"That's a strange word to use, Liz. But then I noticed
that one of us doesn't seem to be in a particularly sane,
intelligent, rational mood here. Now—"

"Now," she agreed. "Open your mouth."

He wasn't breathing at all well. "We'll play this out
until you're tired of it. Until you understand—there's
nothing you can do, Liz. I'm not going to make love
to you."

"Yes. I know." She wouldn't have let him if he'd tried. She was making love to him, not the other way around. All that talking and his lips had separated. Her tongue stole in. His teeth had a way of clamping together when he was demanding control of himself. She ran her tongue along those smooth white teeth. And his tongue... On occasion, Clay's tongue was capable of bluntness, of rash words that he undoubtedly regretted after they were said. Her tongue caressed his tongue.

When it came down to it, Clay was a terribly fallible man. His shoulders had a habit of defensively tightening when he was about to spring in anger. Her fingertips danced over those shoulders. His ears had bad habits of hearing only what they wanted to. When she raised up on the tip of her toes, her lips could reach his ears. She laved the shell with her tongue. Too often Clay hid emotions in those eyes, let people see what they wanted to, not what was there. Her lips brushed his lids closed, so gently. Vulnerable virgins had to be treated gently. Virgins were inevitably afraid of the pain that happened when their defenses were stolen from them, one by one. She loved the man for every mistake he'd made, for every mistake he was going to make. Clay was shuddering.

Wanton, brazen, immoral. The words flashed through her mind and she knew what she was doing, but it didn't feel that way. Giving swelled in her heart, filled her up with a sweet throbbing ache. She'd loved this man forever. But that wasn't what mattered. The value of her love did, because this time, maybe for the first time in her life, she was offering everything she was, honestly, painfully, and to hell with the risks. She'd never been woman enough before, never been strong enough, sure enough.

"Damn you, sunshine...."

Strong and sure were fine, but she couldn't stand on tiptoe forever. She eased down and at the same time her fingers reached for his robe. Her cheek nestled against his furred chest, rubbing, teasing. His body was hotter than a furnace. Her lips researched the heat, flicking over his flat nipples, the slope of his muscled chest. Part of his body was still rock, she noted. But only one part. The part that should be. Her fingers skidded down his taut stomach and discovered tufts of springy hair.

Even giants had their breaking point. Clay's came on an exhale of a harsh breath and a melding of lips that was far more potent than a meeting of the minds. He took her mouth. Blind, angry, he took it as if he'd never encountered a woman's lips before. Hunger and urgency and wicked, wicked pressure. The mattress did a magic thing then. It rose up to meet her back, and Clay was suddenly leaning over her.

His hands touched her face. "I'm so afraid you're going to regret this."

"There isn't a chance on earth I will ever regret this."

"What you do to me, sunshine. What you've always done to me." He shook his head and then kissed her again, his palms sliding down her skin, over throat and breast and belly. Her French tap pants were suddenly gracing the floor.

Her heart had never beat so fast. She'd known before that he was a giving man but had never realized how much. The yellow lamplight shadowed the absorbed concentration in his eyes, the tenderness as his hands sought deliberately to know, to please, to delight. She remembered feeling lost in water and darkness, but this was like being found.

Clay found fragility, as he expected. Vulnerability, which he knew. But her skin. And her scent. And her sweet wildness when her legs wrapped around him, and the soft sounds in her throat. He'd never let it happen before, and maybe this was partly why. Her tongue could wash a man clean of reason. Her hands could make a man forget the past, the present, all time. Her response could make a man believe he could do anything, be anything, have anything.

He wanted to drown in her. His tongue swept the tips of her breasts. His palm stroked her thigh, only gradually, carefully drifting to the more tender flesh on the inside of her leg. The nest of soft springy hair tickled his palm. When he flattened out his hand, she arched to him, all supple, all yielding.

"Clay, I won't break." Her voice was no more than a thread.

But she would. If he was any more careful, any more patient, she knew she would. She slid her hands down to his hips, pressing him closer, the wild in her whispering to the earthy in him. She was not bone china. She was not priceless. She was just…a woman.

What she'd failed to understand for so long was that
was all she wanted to be.

Racked with emotions, she cleaved to him, offering
herself. Helpless. There couldn't be a more powerful
word, a sweeter sensation that being trapped in passion, rich on so much need that she was full with it,
hot with it, dying from it. He covered her and she drew
him inside her, locking him in.

Brown eyes met black. The pulse of rhythm started,
such a fierce primal rhythm that it made no sense no
one had ever been able to write it down. Maybe the
music only belonged between two. Maybe the music
was so intimate it couldn't be captured, except by two.
Between two, it was so easy, so simple. To dance on
sunshine.

# Nine

---

"Where did the fancy lingerie come from?"

"You liked the black satin?"

"No."

Liz chuckled, tilting her head back against Clay's shoulder. "Oh, yes you did."

"You're a dangerous woman."

"Thank you."

"That wasn't necessarily a compliment." His fingers never stopped idly fingering her hair. "There wasn't a man at that party who could keep his eyes off you."

"There wasn't a woman at the party who even tried to keep her hands off you."

"Is that why you arrived at my door at two in the morning dressed like a streaker?"

"Certainly not. I came to deliver a personal thank-you. You're the only one in this entire town who hasn't started a conversation with 'What have you done?' ever since I got my hair cut."

"You always deliver personal thank-yous in that particular fashion?"

"Always."

"Anyway, your hair looks great." He tilted his head critically. Under the dim lamplight, the gold strands bounced around his fingers, all tousled, far too sexy for a sane man's peace of mind. "Especially now."

"See how nice you are?" She leaned up and kissed him, a lingering lazy kiss. "And maybe in four years it will grow out."

"Silly." Her kiss still lingered on his mouth. She should be all kissed out. His gaze dawdled helplessly on her red lips, her sleepy eyes. The first time he had some excuses for losing control. Liz could have tempted a saint. The second time he had no excuses. He'd forgotten to be careful and there had been no thought in his mind beyond possessing her, taking her, claiming her with a fierce wildness and earthy passion that had left his common sense in shambles and the angel in his arms looking shamelessly satisfied and pleased with herself. What was he going to do with her?

"I fibbed," she murmured.

"About what?"

"I didn't come here because you like my hair," she informed him.

"No?" He rearranged the comforter around her chin. She'd already tried to get up twice, and he knew she intended to be gone before Spence wakened. That problem, though he hadn't mentioned it to her, had never happened before. He'd never brought a woman back to sleep here. Yes, she had to leave. But not yet. It was already grating on him that her leaving was necessary. Liz shouldn't be made love to and then left. But then he shouldn't have made love to her at all.

"I came here," Liz told him, "because I wanted to sleep with a wicked man. A bad man. A man with a past, the kind a real lady should avoid. Wasn't that what you were trying to tell me earlier, Clay?"

Uneasily he watched her dislodge the covers yet again and climb on top of him as if he was her own personal mattress. He wasn't prepared to think or talk seriously, not at five in the morning and not after this past night. The feeling of her warm breasts and belly pressed against his did nothing for his concentration. Worse than that, particularly after that last session of lovemaking, her eyes had taken on a dangerously sassy sparkle to add to their glazed sleepiness.

"I have a past of my own, you know," she mentioned conversationally. "I can't figure out how you've misunderstood that for so long. I mean, look, Clay. I've brazenly tried to seduce you three times. What do you think that says about my morals?"

"Nothing. Except that you occasionally get things mixed up."

"I do that," she agreed, her tone light, teasing, coaxing. "A lot. More than that, I've made my share of mistakes. Haircuts. Bad marriages. Wrong career choices. I've hurt people, Clay, in ways that are unforgivable. Did you really think you were the only one?"

"Honey, you are so crazy." His voice was tender, matching the pair of kisses he rained on her forehead, her cheek. "Nothing you are capable of doing in this life is unforgivable, Liz."

"You're wrong."

"I'm right."

"You're bullheaded, I'll give you that. Can I tell you something?"

"No."

She smiled. "Contrary to what I think you want to believe," she said softly, "I am not a mixed-up cookie. I was plenty confused after the separation from my ex-husband, but that was well over a year ago. I have guilts and regrets and grief about that relationship, Clay, but I was never looking for a man to make those feelings easier to take. And images of sex-starved divorcées won't wash either. Based on the sex life I had with my ex-husband, I could have done without for another ten or twenty years." He was trying to talk, trying to interrupt, but she made that difficult by rubbing the tip of her finger over his lips. "Just so it's clear," she said. "I came here because I love you. No other reason."

\* \* \*

At three that afternoon, Liz was standing outside the chamber of commerce office. An ice-blue sky matched a numbingly cold day, and her toes were frozen even from the short walk from the car.

Deep inside her, she was warm enough. Lingering feelings from Clay's lovemaking were furnace warm. All day she'd had the whimsical feeling that strength was flowing through her veins instead of blood. She'd gotten through to Clay. She'd taken the risk, acted on emotion, trusted her feminine instincts. There was a time she'd never believed she could do that.

Loving Clay didn't erase mistakes she'd made. Loving him, though, had taught her that giving wasn't sacrifice. The core of honesty had to do with believing in herself, what she was worth as a woman. Liz had never valued Liz before.

She had every intention of drilling that concept into Clay over a period of time. In fact, she had a great deal she wanted to teach to Clay, but not at this particular moment. Liz had unfinished business to handle first. Dredging up her courage, she pushed open the glass doors and stepped inside.

The front office of the chamber hadn't changed from her last visit and the failed job interview she remembered all too well. The contemporary office decor was done in coral and gray; the woman with her white hair in a bun still had rimless glasses and a smile that was more efficient than welcoming. "Can I help you?"

"Yes. I'm Liz Brady, and I was hoping Mr. Graham might be free."

"Do you have an appointment?"

"I'm afraid not." Typewriters clocked rhythmically in the back. A phone was ringing, just like last time. Last time it hadn't taken Mr. Graham ten minutes to realize she didn't have the public relations degree he wanted. It had taken her less than another ten minutes to quickly, quickly walk out the door, a woman embarrassed that she didn't have the right credentials and mortifyingly aware that what she did have to offer wasn't good enough.

"Well, I'll see," the white-haired woman said, and punched a button on her phone. "Mr. Graham..." A moment later, she said, "Go right in, Miss Brady. I confess he's got quite a schedule this afternoon, but if you won't take up more than fifteen minutes..."

"I won't," Liz promised. She rapped once on the closed gray door, and then walked in. Once the door snapped shut behind her, the office noises became muted.

Mr. Graham sat behind a polished walnut desk. On the short side of fifty, he had laughter lines framing his mouth, and his hair was a brown fluff with a monk's bowl at the crown. His bear-sized frame carried an extra and distinctly huggable twenty pounds. He hadn't been unkind when he'd ushered her out of the office the first time, simply firm.

"I'm sorry to trouble you a second time, Mr. Graham. To tell you the truth, I wasn't sure you'd even be willing to see me again," Liz admitted when he stood up and extended a hand across the desk.

"Nonsense, Miss Brady. I hope there were no hard feelings over that interview? Tell me what I can do for you."

"Did you fill the position?"

"Not yet, but then I think I told you we weren't in a rush. Not that Ravensport couldn't use an immediate shot in the arm, but we assumed it would take several months to find the appropriate person. Sit down, sit down."

"Thank you." She eased out of her coat, but couldn't relax more than to perch at the edge of the chair. She knew her nervousness showed. "It's the job I wanted to talk to you about, Mr. Graham."

"Oh, well..." He looked uncomfortable. She could see his mind ticking off tactful ways to avoid letting her down again, and a little impatience that his secretary hadn't found some way to get him out of this before Liz was in his office.

"Yes," she said gently. "I know you turned me down, and I can't think of anything more awful or awkward than pushing myself where I'm not wanted, but Mr. Graham..." She took a breath. "I feel I did a poor job of representing myself and what qualifications I do have for that position. There isn't a reason on earth why you should listen a second time, but I would appreciate it. I promise I won't take up an hour. I won't even take ten minutes."

She felt his eyes on her face. "I'll listen. But..."

"I don't have your PR degree or communications background. I've also been away from home for ten years, and if you're dead set on hiring someone with

a lot of flash and daring..." She smiled. "I confess I'll
never qualify. The opposite is true. The true nature of
the librarian beast is all—and exactly—what I can offer you. I'm of the breed, Mr. Graham. We're talking
fussy, picky, insatiably nosy. We're talking never
trusting a superficial answer or solution. We're talking about commitment to researching all the corners,
all the options, all the facts, and perfectionists like that
can be a terrible pain to work with. Maybe those don't
initially even sound like job qualifications to you...."

Fifteen minutes later, Mr. Graham, with the oddest
smile on his face, picked up his phone to cancel his
three o'clock appointment. Liz wasn't talking job by
then, she was simply talking her town. Ravensport.
The whole flavor of the community, its unique location, personality and labor force.

The white-haired secretary brought in coffee at 3:45.
Mr. Graham irritably canceled his four o'clock appointment. They were arguing by then, about the kind
of businesses Ravensport really wanted, the kind they
didn't. They were talking water. Lake Michigan was
certainly full of it, and in the summer that lake was
teeming with nice rich boats that Ravensport had
never taken real advantage of. They discussed a place
to moor those boats in the winter, a small marina,
maybe even a boat-building business. "Good boats,
fancy stuff, quality workmanship," Mr. Graham
murmured. "That's exactly the kind of thing we
need."

At four-thirty they were still talking carpenters and
capital. At five o'clock, the white-haired secretary

poked her head in the door to announce she was going home. It was obvious from her expression that Liz had destroyed her entire well-organized afternoon of appointments for Mr. Graham.

Once she was gone, Mr. Graham turned to Liz with a sigh. "She's a dragon. You'll have to find your own ways of making peace with her once you start working. I've never been very good at it."

"I wonder if there's a book on it," Andy said musingly an hour later. The spaghetti in front of him was cold, the garlic toast was burned and he'd forgotten dressing for the salad. He'd also nearly forgotten what it was like to make dinner himself, but it wasn't his fault Liz had been spoiling him for the past month.

"A book on what?"

"A book on how to peel sisters off the walls. What are you getting up for now?"

"Napkins," Liz said self-righteously.

"While you're up, it might occur to you to take off your coat."

"I'm going to Clay's right after dinner."

"Somehow that doesn't surprise me. You going to float over there or just drive like regular mortals?" With all due patience, Andy accepted the fork she handed him and the kiss she plopped on his forehead. Then he got up himself for the napkins. "I'm not sure what all the excitement's about. You said the job wouldn't seriously start for another month."

She nodded. "That's when the chamber budgeted the start of the job, but that hardly matters, Andy. I need a couple weeks to go back to Milwaukee, finish packing up and close the apartment, find someone to sublet."

"That's the first rational thing you've said since you walked in," Andy observed. "While we're on a roll, let's go with it. Sleep."

"Sleep."

"Sleep," Andy repeated. "Did you have in mind getting any before Christmas? I happened to notice that you seemed to be coming in this morning at the same time I was getting up."

"I did come in rather late," Liz murmured.

"Call it dawn, give or take a few minutes." He added conversationally, "I've known Clay a heck of a long time. I've also watched this chalk and cheese relationship develop between the two of you since you were in pigtails. I never understood it, and for God's sake don't try to explain it now." He looked alarmed when Liz opened her mouth. "I don't want to know. A man's just slightly inclined to be nervous when he notices his sister drowning in quicksand."

"Andy!" Liz was stunned. Her brother was actually dabbling in a little emotional territory. Completely out of character.

"I love that man like a brother," Andy said quietly, "but Clay has been like quicksand for women from the day he was born. And that's all I'm going to say. Except that I hope you know what you're doing."

"I do," she said simply.

She couldn't doubt it. It had been just that kind of day, when doubts seemed miles away and nothing could dent the exhilaration heated inside of her. The job mattered. It mattered that she'd stood up for herself, because she desperately wanted work that involved people, commitment, and was something she could sink her teeth into. To a lesser degree, the job mattered because of Clay.

Clay had always been drawn to protect the impulsive, the vulnerable, the foolish and fallible. She had no illusions that was how he'd seen her as a teenager, and how he'd seen her when she first came home. To cure Clay of his overprotective tendencies would take time—more than a carefully spoken talk that morning, more than a simple job. Those things were beginnings, though. Ways of showing him that she was not a woman who needed sheltering, but an equal. A woman capable of mistakes but also of fighting her own battles, who knew her own mind and put a value on her feelings and instincts, and on herself.

She left the dishes for her brother—who looked appropriately pained—and drove to the motel at celebration speed. Clay would be busy, of course. She had in mind only a quick sharing of triumphs and lavishing the kind of kiss that had been building all day, but her whimsical mood faded when she pulled in the parking lot.

Two police cars were parked by the back doors of the motel. A small crowd had gathered in the doorway, heads and coats blocking her view. Whatever the source of noise and confusion, common sense told her to avoid adding to it. Her heels clicked a face pace toward the front doors, until she noticed a red-capped urchin hiding in the bushes. He'd remembered a hat and coat, but hadn't any shoes, and his stocking feet were bouncing on top of each other on the wet ground. When he saw her, Spence came flying. "You won't believe it! It's terrific, Liz! We have a thief!" he enthused.

"Wonderful," Liz murmured dryly. She swooped him up and delivered a hug. "Why do I have the feeling that your dad's positive you're locked in a room with Cameron?"

"Playing gin rummy. But Cam fell asleep in front of the TV and then I saw these lights flashing by the windows, and—"

"Tell me once we get you inside and into dry socks, kiddo."

"I can't leave now. They're just getting him. And my dad hit the guy. You should have seen him, Liz!" Spence slid to his feet and mimicked the moves of a foot-prancing prizefighter, Slam with his right hook, Jam with his left, all the way down the long corridor to his room. "This lady was crying—see, it was her necklace. And I guess the guy she checked in with was her brother, but her brother had this big problem. The kind of problem like when they put on TV 'the following program is not suitable for kids.' Heck, I know what that means."

"Socks?" His "heck" inevitably brought a grin. Clay's campaign was finally working...though in the meantime Clay's son's teeth were chattering. His two wet socks had been stashed by the door, but he was too excited to worry about dry replacements.

"In my room, naturally. Anyway, we all know that's drugs. You know what I'm going to say when somebody asks me if I want to try drugs, don't you?"

"No, honey, what?" She found one long white and one long gray sock, both of which were at least dry.

"No way, José. Buzz off, buster. Drugs are not fun, stupid—that's what I'm going to say. And if they keep bugging me, I'm going to punch them out just like my dad punched that guy. Wham! See, this lady was trying to get her necklace back and the brother kind of got mad at her. My dad says nobody hits a lady. Not ever, no exceptions, no talk, no excuses. Even if it's Sarah Breeling and she steals your best eraser. And then the police came! Two cars!"

"I saw." Liz basically understood, though Spence's version was rather garbled, highly dramatic and blissfully excited. Dry-socked and shoed, he had to repeat the entire story for Cameron, who'd wakened from his catnap long enough to panic at the loss of his charge. Cam immediately went out to see for himself what had happened and what he could do, once he was certain Spence was safely stashed with Liz.

Spence was safely stashed, but as an hour passed his mood changed from elated manic to pit low and exhausted. "You know what's going to happen when Dad comes back, don't you?"

"He's going to wonder what you're still doing up past nine o'clock at night?"

"Not that. We're going to get the lecture."

"The lecture?" The couch was four cushions wide. Spence deemed it essential that he share the same square with her. Post-nine o'clock Liz had discovered before that he wasn't opposed to a cuddle, even if it was with a girl.

"The lecture. About how we have to move because this isn't a good place for me. And you're not going to tell him about Cam's little nap, are you? Dad will have a fit. I keep trying to tell him I'm no kid anymore."

"I know you do."

"But he gets overupset about things. Like the bar. I mean, what's the big deal? He doesn't want me near the place because my grandma used to have a problem. I don't go near the place. Who'd want to? And if we didn't have the bar, we couldn't have George. George needs a son, see, and even though I'm dad's son I sometimes loan myself out to George. Heck, what else could I do, he's all alone. Did you decide?"

Spence's steady monologue had been increasingly interrupted by blatant, noisy yawns. By the time the question came up, his words were starting to slur and his eyes were at half-mast.

"Did I decide what, sport?" She smoothed back his hair, loving him even if his elbow was sticking in her ribs.

"About us. If you're not going to marry me, are you going to marry my dad? You said you'd give me an answer the next time I saw you."

"Did I?"

"Yup."

"Well . . ." Those lids of his were almost down. "Is it okay if I just love both you and your dad for today?" she asked helplessly.

"That's no good. I already knew that," he said disgustedly. "And I'm not going to sleep."

"No?"

He was a deadweight in her arms for the next half hour, far too heavy to lift and far too sweet to move. Liz only glanced up when she finally heard the doorknob turn.

Strain shadowed Clay's eyes. She could tell in a look that he was tight and tense. No one needed a business crisis after a long day and a sleepless night. "Excitement finally over with?" she whispered sympathetically.

He raised his eyes to the ceiling as if to express exasperation with life in general, then crossed the room to scoop up his son. For an instant his eyes flashed on hers and last night shimmered between them like lover's lightning, something silver and bright and hot. Quickly, that look was gone and a mask seemed to drop over Clay's expression. He was tired, she reminded herself.

When he strode toward Spence's room to put the little one to bed, she stood up, suddenly restless. I am not uneasy, she told herself. What is there to be uneasy about? She stretched to release all the cramped muscles that only an eight-year-old curled up at your side could produce. She thought about the job she could hardly wait to come here and tell Clay about. She thought about everything they'd shared the night before, of futures. And she decided wryly that it wasn't the time. Clay returned from Spence's room and threw himself on the couch like a man too tired to breathe.

"I take it you heard the story?"

"Yes."

"Hell." Legs sprawled, he leaned his head back. "Whether anyone in this town wants to believe it or not, I thought I had a pretty decent place here. A place where families stop, where families want to eat and stay. Even the bar—sure, we encourage singles, but not hangouts, not pickups, not troublemakers. But then something like this happens, and when it comes right down to it, this is just no place to raise a kid."

"Spence said you'd have that reaction."

"The kid's too smart for his own good."

"I think he's got his head put on just fine, and what happened tonight could have happened anywhere," Liz said soothingly. "Come on, Clay. You can find muggers in the best neighborhoods and the worst, a high rise in Milwaukee or a backwater farm in Wisconsin's cheese country." She moved behind him and gently nudged his head forward as she would for a child. Her fingers rubbed the tight muscles in his nape. "I know you want to protect Spence, but there's no way to totally protect a child from life unless you plan on raising him on a desert island. Besides, it isn't what he's exposed to that's going to make a difference in what kind of grown man he turns into. It's how he's raised, how he's taught to react and think and value what he knows."

"Yeah? Well, I don't seem to do such a cracker-jack job of that either. Don't, Liz." He eased forward. She suddenly found her fingers in midair and a streak of unreasonable hurt pulsing through her. She knew he was tired to beat the band, but it hurt nonetheless.

"I'll make a pot of coffee," she said swiftly.

"No."

"A beer sound better?"

"What I want," he said flatly, "is a little space. It's been a hell of a day. Coffee isn't going to cut it, and neither is the canned lecture my son set you up to say." He glanced up and swore under his breath, seeing the expression in her eyes. "I didn't mean that. Wait a minute."

She was groping, fast, for her coat, eyes down and her heart coming apart. "I've got to go. Really, I was only staying until you came back for Spence."

"No, you weren't."

"I'm just as tired as you are," she continued swiftly. "Heavens, nobody gets as short-tempered as I do on short sleep. Talk about tactless on my part."

He didn't catch up with her until she was halfway to the door, and then he was simply there, blocking her path, his palm touching her cheek and his callused hand trying to prop up her chin. "You couldn't be tactless the day hell turned into an iceberg. Look at me, sunshine."

Her view was blurry because of the silly tears. They were silly. How many hours had the man been on his feet? And she wasn't the type to cave in for a cross word. But after last night, she'd been so sure of welcome. She'd been so sure that he'd want and need her there exactly when he was tired and stressed out.

His face was graven still, dark eyes hollow and bleak. "I loved the little lecture. And I loved your being here when I walked in. I love the way Spence thinks the world rises and sets with you, and I can't think of a woman in hell I've ever needed. Not like you, sunshine."

"Oh, Clay."

He shook his head. "But if you think I'm going to take advantage of you again... No." He repeated, "Just no, Liz."

"Take advantage—"

"Don't look like that. That's what happened last night and we both know it. You were... in a mood. Maybe I've always been in that same damn mood every time I've been around you, and maybe it was always going to come to that point sometime. Of making love. Of finding out exactly how it was going to be between us."

She had a terrible time finding the words. "And you found out."

"I found out. That you're innocent, vulnerable. That you're softer than yellow roses. That you'd give and give and give. But not to me. Because I also found out what it was like to wake up, feeling like I'd used you, like I'd taken advantage of someone who was precious to me, someone who trusted me. Everything that happened today... I looked at my life..." He shook his head. "Go home, Liz."

"Clay—" When had the day turned into an empty nightmare?

"When you leave here, I'm going to get Cameron for Spence, and I'm going to go to the bar. You know the singer there, Char. She's the kind of woman I've always had in my life, Liz. Like belongs with like. She's been around the block twice, and hell, so have I. So..."

She didn't need to hear any more.

# Ten

Liz wrapped another glass in newspaper, then plopped it in the waiting packing box with total disregard to its future. She'd never liked those glasses anyway. Next to the cupboard was a white phone. She'd been in Milwaukee ten days now. Long enough to handle her banking and business, to start searching for a tenant to sublet the apartment, and to see old friends and begin the process of packing up for a permanent move. Long enough for that darn phone to ring.

It hadn't. Not that she'd expected Clay to call. He was undoubtedly busy with his motel and restaurant, with Spence, with rebuilding that one-against-the-world shell she'd made the mistake of denting.

Men! She slid plates clattering on top of plates in another box, making lonesome noises in an apartment that was already too hollow with quiet. Her yellow couch and chairs had sold almost before she put the ad in the paper. Pictures and books had already been packed and were ready to ship to Ravensport. If it was going to take a few more days to clear up the last details of moving, then she didn't need more than a bed and a few dishes to camp out in the meantime.

Ignoring the plates, she paced through the nearly empty living room toward her bedroom. Snow was scurrying in the windowsills, hiding from a nasty November wind. When she'd moved into the place after her divorce, she'd been little more than an injured animal. She'd wanted nothing more than to lick her wounds and hide from life. She'd done exactly that for a year. Blame was a self-feeding companion. It had taken going home to Ravensport for her to be able to forgive herself, to take that tumble back into life and stop beating herself with guilt. Instead, she'd learned to use the mistakes she'd made to grow and change.

It had taken going home to learn honesty—and to fall in love with a man who didn't like that word. For instance, Liz had met Clay's singer more than once. The lady was a voluptuous looker with a sultry smile and a no-question crush on Clay, but Char—to be kind—had limited mentality. Clay never tolerated boredom well.

So he'd hurt Liz to get her out of his life. Fine. She was out. She paced back out of the bedroom, glared at the phone and resumed her packing. Canned goods this time. Soups. Three cans of tomato, three of mushroom. How had she ended up with eight French onion?

Tagalong-Liz echoed in her mind. How often she'd thrown herself at him rang in her mind. How many thousands of mistakes she'd made where Clay was concerned. But none of them as idiotic as his. The words echoed in her mind. You'll find the right man, Liz. A good man. And as far as that nonsense about his taking advantage of her...

It all boiled down to the same thing. He was a man who hadn't forgiven himself those major mistakes that came with life. He hadn't let emotional honesty in yet and didn't believe in himself. She'd worn all those shoes—never mind that hers were 7AA and his were 11s.

She finished off the packing box with cake and Jell-O mixes, then stretched with utter laziness and stalked over to the phone. Eight punches on the dial, and then it rang. Once, twice. She thought about honesty, she really did. White lies didn't really dent that. Three times, four. In fact to be absolutely honest, lies were occasionally necessary. Well, lies weren't necessary, but love was, and that was what honesty was all about: admitting what mattered, welcoming the risks, fighting if it came to it. Once more. Only once more. One more try, Clay Stewart because I'm so damned lonely and everything you did makes me believe you love me. Five rings and then six—her lungs exhaled relief when the receiver was picked up.

"Andy? It's Liz. Listen, bro, I have to ask you to do me a favor...."

*Getting Married.*

And everyone on Interstate 43 seemed to think this was a holiday. Clay passed yet another set of Sunday drivers and smashed his foot on the accelerator. By the time he reached the outskirts of Milwaukee, his temper was marginal and his nerves were frayed. He didn't know the city, which didn't help.

Once he was in stoplight traffic, he had a few seconds to repair his appearance in the rearview mirror. The suit he owned solely for funerals and weddings didn't look bad. In fact, the dark blue made him look like a confident, self-possessed, commanding man in full control. The striped shirt, though, looked as if it had been ironed on the expressway. Unconsciously he must have unknotted the tie; it had a drunken loop. His hair looked hand-shoveled. The comb he always carried in his back pocket had disappeared. He fixed what he could until he turned down Merriweather. Liz's street.

Getting Married.

3421 Merriweather. He found it, but there wasn't a parking place closer than a block away from the two-story brick building. The short walk gave him the chance to erase the brooding frown from his face and practice a casual, calm expression. The same expression he'd adopted when Andy had stopped over that morning to tell him the news, the same expression he'd put on when Spence had asked bewilderedly, "Dad? Why are you putting on a suit?"

Spence could ask the most irritating questions. Clay didn't know why he was wearing the suit. A man sometimes got in the mood, that was all, just as a man sometimes liked to drive expressways like a bat out of hell. You are going to be calm. Friendly, concerned, rational. You just happened to be in Milwaukee this afternoon and you'd heard she was *Getting Married.* Clay pushed open the door and let himself into the brightly lit lobby with dark red carpeting. Four apartments; one of them was hers. 3421 happened to be the far door at the end of the second floor, which was where his feet suddenly lodged in stubborn silence. The day was freezing. His body registered firecracker hot. He could have run a marathon with the dark, fierce energy coiled up inside him. His throat was dry, his head thick, and the tips of his fingers were blue and shaky with cold.

He shoveled those fingers through his hair and then knocked. *Knock, dammit, do not pound. We are perfectly calm.* When there was no immediate answer, he considered tearing down the door. But then the knob twisted from the other side.

"Clay!"

Another time it might have occurred to Clay that she should have been more surprised to see him. At the moment he was too busy noticing Liz. She was barefoot. A pair of old jeans hugged her slim hips and a loose baggy sweater buried her figure in yellow. Her hair was tousled, her skin without makeup. Her eyes danced with sparkle and her lips tilted in an easy welcoming smile. She looked rested, calm, happy.

He could have strangled her. "Hope you don't mind an impromptu visit? I had to drive to Milwaukee, so I thought I'd stop by."

"Wonderful, come on in! Although I have to admit the place is a mess. I'm still in the middle of packing up, Clay. Just step over everything, I've got a pot of coffee on the stove."

"Great," he enthused. If she dared ask him why he had driven to Milwaukee, he hadn't the least idea what he was going to tell her. At the moment he didn't want to tell her anything. He wanted his hands swallowed in her yellow hair and his mouth erasing her calm smile.

"Moving's a terrible pain. I was only in this place a year and I can't believe how much nonsense I accumulated."

He followed her to the narrow kitchen where she reached up on tiptoe for two mugs. The movement tightened the muscles in his thighs and bottom. His jaw refused to function until she turned back with a smile and handed him a steaming mug. "Heard you were getting married," he said heartily, and could have kicked a cupboard. He sounded like Santa Claus booming out good cheer.

"Yes. Andy told you?"

"He mentioned it." He took one sip of the brew and put the mug on the counter. It was either that or pitch it.

She gave a small, light laugh. "Clay, I'm afraid if I don't keep at this I'm never going to finish it."

"Fine, fine. Keep doing whatever you're doing—what's he like?"

"Who?"

"This man you're going to marry."

"Oh . . ." She pulled out a drawer under the counter, the drawer that exists in every kitchen for catchalls. She stepped blithely around boxes to find the one she was looking for, and then started feeding it hand can openers and hammers and screwdrivers and pencils and keys and a corkscrew. "He's a wonderful man, Clay, you'd like him very much."

"You've only been back here eleven days." Twelve hours and thirty-seven minutes, he mentally added.

"But I knew him for a long time before this," Liz said blithely.

"How long?"

"Years."

"That's nice. That's very nice," Clay said reasonably. "So what the hell does he do?"

"For a living? He works with people. He's wonderful with people, very sensitive and caring. The kind of man people naturally look up to."

She disappeared. He followed her, negotiating around boxes and debris on the floor in the living room. Her bedroom was small. The only thing still in it was a brass bed. He stared at its rumpled sheets.

"How's Char?" she asked blithely.

"Char who?" She was bent over again, taking things out of drawers. Pale yellow things and pale pink things and all he could do was stare at her turned-up bottom, her spine, the hair wisping on her cheeks.

"Don't you think—" He took the belligerent rage out of his tone and cleared his throat, then tried again. "Don't you think you decided to get married a little *quickly*?"

"Not really, Clay. Like I said, I've known him for a long time before this. I think I've always known." Just for a moment she rocked back on her heels and her eyes took on a dreamy expression. "I've always known he was a man to grow old with, a man to want children by. He's so good, Clay. The best of men. The kind of man you would trust with your life."

"Swell," Clay snapped.

"And he needs me." Her face tilted up to his with a whimsical smile. "He's the kind of man who'd be there when the chips were down, but even more important than that . . . I guess as a woman I just need to feel needed, too."

"I'm glad you feel needed."

"I knew you would be."

He spit out the words. "I couldn't be more thrilled for you."

"You know something?" she asked softly. "I thought that would be your reaction. You kept telling me I'd find the right man, sometime, and he's so wonderful, Clay."

Something snapped. Maybe everything snapped, his head, his heart, his bones, all of Clay. There wasn't a time he'd ever thought he could treat Liz roughly, and he certainly didn't mean to, but his hands were suddenly on her arms, tugging her up to him. One hand

locked the back of her head and the other swept down
and held her as his mouth claimed hers.

Like a match on an oil slick, that physical contact
set off an explosion of fire. Her lips molded under his
as if they belonged to him. He took in her scent, her
taste, her softness. He took in, then he took. His head
reeled. He knew he was holding her with bruising
pressure, but couldn't let up. The ache inside him was
bigger than the sky, terrifying in its desperate and un-
appeasable intensity. The only thing he could hold on
to was Liz.

As if there was some sunshine left in a world gone
black, he felt her fingers in his hair, her small breasts
cushioning his chest, the heat and warmth flooding
through her. She was responding. He forced his head
up, his voice little more than a rasp. "You think that
man of yours makes you feel fire like this?"

"Every..." She was breathless. "Every time he
touches me."

"No." The word wrenched from him, hollow and
despairing.

"Every time," she echoed. "And you ought to
know, Clay."

"What?"

"I said you ought to know. Heaven knows I've
never been able to keep my hands off you for more
than two minutes at a time since I first met you." He
looked utterly confused, old with anxiety, tense with
despair. His hair was such a mess. His tie looked like
a fourteen-year-old-boy's first efforts. She moved to

straighten it, and then simply unlooped it and dragged it off his neck.

"Sunshine..."

"Don't you sunshine me!" If she'd loved him any less, she might have been tempted to use the tie to strangle him. He'd shown up, which told her all she needed to know about Clay Stewart's feelings for Elizabeth Brady. If her heart was soaring, though, her hands were still shaking. Not because she was unsure or afraid, but because she was furious.

"You've been under this stupid illusion for a long time that I don't know my own mind, Clay. That I need someone to protect me from making foolish, impulsive decisions. That I'm incapable of exercising good judgment." She poked her finger in his chest. "Let me tell you something, buster. I have excellent judgment, and particularly excellent judgment in men. I goofed up once, yes. I'm not perfect, but I know a good man when I see one. You're the one who doesn't." She poked him again. "I don't love losers, Clay. Life's too damned short and I don't have that kind of time to waste. Not anymore. I'm not settling for less than one man, the best man, and it's about time you got around to believing it—don't argue with me!"

"Liz..." Good heavens, who would have guessed his brown-eyed angel could turn into such a shrew? His Sunshine was slightly out of control. Tears were spattering from her eyes. Her hands were waving wildly. She was actually yelling.

"And another thing—"

Clay had no more time for "another thing." He'd
nearly lost the only woman who'd ever believed in
him. He knew he'd come here to kidnap her from the
man she thought she was marrying, and that wasn't
the honorable thing to do—not if she had found the
right man, a good man. Never mind. Honor and Clay
Stewart had never been blood brothers. Then his head
finally registered that there'd been no other man.

There would be no other man, and while his lady
was slightly out of control, he thought he'd tactfully
introduce that into the conversation. Hell. Skip the
conversation.

His mouth touched hers and his fingers slid down to
the snap on her jeans. Her heart was beating fast, but
then so was his. She'd nearly given him heart failure,
and he had the terrible feeling he wasn't going to be
able to make this go slow and patient and tender, the
way Liz should be made love to. Some things just
wouldn't wait.

He had to be positive she understood that he desperately loved her. That he desperately needed her.

He couldn't, wouldn't ever give her up. Right or
wrong, bad or good, tough times or good ones, he
couldn't, that was all. He'd tried to, but he was never
going to be that strong. He pulled her jeans down her
thighs and calves. He tugged off the sweater. And
suddenly he had the skin that needed Clay's brand-
ing.

She fumbled with his buttons, pushed off his coat,
fumbled with more buttons, tugged at his belt. She felt
the rough pressure of his mouth, the arrogant sweep

of his tongue, his trembling hands, his whole body shuddering under her touch. Her tough, protective man was coming apart at the seams. The skilled lover had forgotten his skills.

She didn't want the skills. She wanted the weight of him covering her. She wanted to drag kisses over every inch of his skin until he couldn't think, couldn't breathe, until he had no more doubts about her, about him, about anything. She wanted the vulnerable Clay inside her. What if he hadn't come? "Let me," she whispered fiercely.

His hands were everywhere, in his way. Limbs tangled every which way when he eased her down to the mattress. Hot and urgent, his mouth pressed on hers, too hard, he knew. Her fingers were racing over his chest, which did nothing for control he'd already lost. Her hips surged against him. His lips skidded down, found a lace bra he'd forgotten to remove. He pushed it aside, his lips finding vulnerable white breasts, taut and hard with wanting. Not taut enough. Not hard enough.

He loved her. His mouth dipped to her smooth flat belly, and felt the clutch of her fingers when he strayed lower. He loved the sweet mound of honey-colored hair, and he loved her collarbones. He loved her fingernails and her smiles. He loved her in pastels and in red; he loved her with her mouth full of oysters. He had to be sure she knew and understood that no matter what mistakes he'd made, no matter what rough roads he'd traveled, what he felt for Liz was good. Right. The best of everything he was.

"Come to me, Clay." She urged him up with whispers, kisses, fingers, touch. Her very strong, hard man had diamonds in his eyes. She took him inside her, all she could do, all that made sense.

"I adore you, sunshine."

"Not adore," she whispered. "Love. Just love me, and keep on loving me."

His lips promised. Suddenly, there were fast swift soft kisses, all over her face. Whispers about love and need and the terrible terrible fear that he'd lost her tumbled from his lips. She tried to talk but couldn't. Her hips lifted to match the contractions racking through his body. The rippling, pagan rhythm was like soaring through space, soaring through darkness—but not alone. A hot, wet, bright star enclosed them, shooting free and wild toward ecstasy.

Her heart was never going to be the same. Her lashes closed, arms wrapped around his warm body, she kept thinking that her heart was going to have to slow down sometime. Clay tried to shift and her hands tightened. "Don't you dare move," she whispered.

"I'm too heavy."

"No, you're not."

"Sunshine..." He eased his head slightly away from her. Bold daylight danced over her limbs, intimately shining on skin he loved. "You're going to have to marry me."

Her eyes opened and she tilted her head. "Not that," she whispered. "Not a fate worse than death. Not—"

He grinned, the first grin he'd felt in about eleven days, thirteen hours and forty-seven minutes. For that sass, he leaned over and kissed her silly. She responded with dangerous, willful, impulsive enthusiasm, but he wanted more than that. "Say yes," he ordered her gruffly.

"Are you going to work hard on this overprotective streak of yours?" she asked sternly.

"Yes."

"Have you finally got it through your head that I'm a brilliantly intelligent, capable, beautiful woman who knows what she's doing with her life?"

"Sweetheart, I knew that a long time ago. I even knew how humble you were."

"Have you finally figured out that you're the most brilliant, loving, caring, perceptive man who ever lived?" Her voice hushed. "Dammit, you have to see it, Clay. Everyone makes mistakes. Yours never made you less, but more. You grew. You changed."

"Because of you. Because a long time ago a pigtailed girl believed I was better than I was, so I had to try to be."

"No. Because of you. Because you're the best."

"Sweetheart, just say yes before I go out of my mind."

"We're going to have to have all boys," Liz said dismally. "If we have girls, I figure you'll have them in a convent before they're out of diapers. Or else between you and Spence, they'll be so spoiled rotten that no one can live with them. Only boys, Clay."

"Sunshine, if you don't say yes within the next three and a half seconds—" He frowned, trying to think of an adequate threat. That Liz was looking at him with interest and anticipation didn't help.

She touched his cheek, smoothing the tough line of his jaw with her fingertip. Clay was a man who needed a guardian, she thought fleetingly. Strong men were the most vulnerable. She'd have to watch after him most preciously for the next thousand years. She'd have to work on making him believe in himself, and she knew darn well it was going to take time for him to outgrow his tendency to overprotect those he loved. They'd fight. A lot. They'd make mistakes, but she was no longer afraid of that. People couldn't grow and change unless they occasionally floundered and failed.

"Elizabeth." She was sliding a leg over his body, shifting her weight on top of his. Her smile was a brood when she felt the reaction of his body to the length of hers. Elbows on both sides of his face, she offered him a king-of-the-castle kiss. He had the terrible feeling that he'd been better off when she was a kid and had a hero-worship crush on him. That smile of hers was pure woman's. She knew him too well. She knew exactly who he was, the kind of man he was, and the damned fool woman seemed to love him anyway. What else could he do but put his arms around her?

"I love you, Clay."

Looking as smug as a cat with the cream, he shook his head in despair. She dipped down and took a most unladylike bite of his shoulder. "Honey, would you

just say yes before I completely forget the question?"
he asked desperately.

"There aren't any questions between us, love."

"Even so—"

"Yes. Yes. Yes. Yes. Yes."

*     *     *     *     *

# Take 4 Silhouette Romance novels & a surprise gift

# FREE

Then preview 6 brand-new Silhouette Romance novels—delivered to your door as soon as they come off the presses! If you decide to keep them, pay just $1.95* each, *with no shipping, handling or other charges of any kind!*

Each month, you'll meet lively young heroines and share in their thrilling escapes, trials and triumphs... virile men you'll find as attractive and irresistible as the heroines do... and colorful supporting characters you'll feel you've always known.

Start with 4 Silhouette Romance novels and a surprise gift absolutely FREE. They're yours to keep without obligation. You can always return a shipment and cancel at any time.

Simply fill out and return the coupon today!

*$1.70 each plus 69¢ postage and handling per shipment in Canada.

*Silhouette Romance®*

---

### Clip and mail to: Silhouette Books

**In U.S.:**
901 Fuhrmann Blvd.
P.O. Box 9013
Buffalo, NY 14240-9013

**In Canada:**
P.O. Box 609
Fort Erie, Ontario
L2A 5X3

**YES!** Please rush me 4 FREE Silhouette Romance novels and my free surprise gift. Then send me 6 new Silhouette Romance novels to preview each month as soon as they come off the presses. Bill me at the low price of $1.95* each with no shipping, handling or other hidden costs. There is no minimum number of books I must purchase. I can always return a shipment and cancel at any time. Even if I never buy another book from Silhouette Romance, the 4 free novels and the surprise gift are mine to keep forever.

*$1.70 each plus 69¢ postage and handling per shipment in Canada.

215 BPL BP7F

| | | |
|---|---|---|
| Name | (please print) | |
| Address | | Apt. |
| City | State/Prov. | Zip/Postal Code |

This offer is limited to one order per household and not valid to present subscribers. Price is subject to change.

SilR-SUB-1D

# COMING NEXT MONTH

## AVAILABLE NOW:

**COMING NEXT MONTH**

# Silhouette Classics

### The best books from the past by your favorite authors.

*The first two stories of a delightful collection . . .*

### #1 DREAMS OF EVENING by Kristin James

As a teenager, Erica had given Tonio Cruz all her love, body and soul, but he betrayed and left her anyway. Ten years later, he was back in her life, and she quickly discovered that she still wanted him. But the situation had changed—now she had a son. A son who was very much like his father, Tonio, the man she didn't know whether to hate—or love.

### #2 INTIMATE STRANGERS by Brooke Hastings

Rachel Grant had worked hard to put the past behind her, but Jason Wilder's novel about her shattered her veneer of confidence. When they met, he turned her life upside down again. Rachel was shocked to discover that Jason wasn't the unfeeling man she had imagined. Haunted by the past, she was afraid to trust him, but he was determined to write a new story about her—one that had to do with passion and tenderness and love.